Wahnayah

By

Doug Gollihar

PublishAmerica
Baltimore

First printing

ISBN: 1-4137-9552-8
PUBLISHED BY PUBLISHAMERICA, LLLP
www.publishamerica.com
Baltimore

Printed in the United States of America

I dedicate this book in loving memory
of my son Donald, who was killed in
1996 in an automobile accident.
He was part Choctaw.

Also to the great Native American
Tribes of the Northwest.
Tlingit, Nootka, Kutchin,
Chipewyan, Kwakiutl, and Yellowknife.
To all Native Americans who have
Struggled to maintain their identity
In a changing world.

Chapter 1

It was a cloudy, rainy, dreary day when he came into the railway station in San Francisco. San Francisco was a young booming town with a population of maybe 800 people. Since the gold rush many back east had rushed west to California. San Francisco was a rough and tough town with little law other than a man's gun. Clede McCabe had joined the army looking for adventure but what he found was anything but adventure. The gold in the rivers wasn't what he was looking for; it was the frontier in the Northwest where a man could be alone with nature, that's what he yearned for. The war had been a bloody affair with a lack of excitement that he had joined expecting to find. Three years of managing to stay alive left him drained. He wanted to get away somewhere quiet where he could think and find peace of mind. He boarded a train out of Indianapolis bound for San Francisco. It had been a very long trip from his farm in Indiana to San Francisco but Clede wasn't in any hurry. The sale of his father's farm had given him enough money to finally seek out his lifelong dream. He always wanted to see the far Northwest, maybe even go to Alaska. The Northwest was raw and untouched by white men other than a few fur traders. He had taken a bullet to the leg from a young sniper during his last few weeks in the army. It was just his luck. The kid was barely sixteen years old. If he had known he was just a kid, he wouldn't have been so quick on the trigger, but how could he know it was just a kid. Under the cover of darkness you shot first and asked questions later. Heck, he hated that war with a passion and what it had done to him. Many of his friends had lost legs, arms and been permanently maimed but he had been lucky, the bullet had just missed the bone. His leg was doing better every day but he still walked with a slight limp, the muscle tissue hadn't completely healed as of yet. As he walked along he remembered the carnage and terror of it all. He thought to himself, *There are no real winners in a war, we all lost.* As he glanced out at the Pacific Ocean and the beautiful blue waters a peacefulness warmed his insides. Why did men fight wars? he pondered. Killing and mutilating each other over things that just didn't make much sense.

After spending a day in San Francisco, to rest up, he caught a boat early the next morning that sailed up the coast to a settlement called Alki Point. Two days of being tossed around in that boat was enough of the sea life for him. After they anchored in the harbor he collected his few belongings and rode the lifeboat to the shore. Alki Point really wasn't much more than a trading post where the fur trappers, Indians, and a few gold miners could come and get supplies or sell their wares. Slinging his bag over his shoulder, that contained everything he owned in this world, he stepped out of the lifeboat onto the muddy bank that led to the street. A makeshift building had been crudely put together and had a poorly painted sign that read "The White Rose Saloon." A couple of rough, plump skimpily dressed women looked out the door toward him as he made his way up the street. They were probably the only women in these parts. A couple of prostitutes who found the business booming and the competition was very scarce. They weren't much to look at but life was hard, they had to be tough to survive and the men here would spend all they had for a night with one of them. On the left side of the street he noticed the Wilson Hotel, along with a restaurant next door, these were the only well-built buildings in the settlement. On the right side there was the trading post. The rest of the structures at the outskirts of town were makeshift tents. He decided to start at the trading post first and get the supplies he would need for his journey north through the mountains. Making his way to the store he stepped up on the rough wooden walkway. He cleaned his boots on the edge of the weathered board the best he could, stomped his feet some and entered the store. A tall lanky man with a red plaid shirt a face full of beard smiled with a mouth full of missing teeth. The man nodded and welcomed him into the store. The man said his name was Bill and asked Clede, "What can I do for ya, stranger."

Clede hesitated a moment as his eyes scanned the room, then he said, "I need a good rifle, hatchet, matches, ammunition, and enough flour and salt to hold me over for at least a couple of months."

Clede's eyes caught sight of a heavy bear coat and a black mountain hat. He asked Bill if those were for sale. Bill grinned and said everything you see in here is for sale for the right price. Then Bill replied, "I noticed you're wearing a uniform. How's the war going?" Clede stared at him with his cold blue eyes and said nothing. The storekeeper could tell by the look on his face he had hit on a sore subject with the stranger. He turned and laid the hat and coat on the table between him and Clede. Then turned back to fill the request for supplies that Clede had quoted to him.

Clede screwed the hat down on his head; it fit a little tight but it would stretch, it was made of leather. Soon Bill had the supplies packed and asked Clede if he wanted him to store them in the back of the store until he was ready for them or did he want to take them with him? Clede replied, "Yes, hold them, I won't need them till I leave tomorrow. I'll be by early in the mornin' to pick them up."

Without speaking another word he turned and walked back on to the street, jumping back suddenly as a wagon passed by splattering mud and manure on his boots that drained down the sloping street. Grumbling to himself he wiped the mud from his boots, on the back of his pant legs, then headed for the restaurant. His stomach growled with hunger pains, it had been nearly two days since he had eaten. The train ticket and supplies had taken most of the money he had left. He looked up the street and located the restaurant next door to the Wilson Hotel; he walked slowly along the wooden walkway until he stood in front of the restaurant door. Grabbing the doorknob he opened the door and entered. Standing at the door he looked around the room. He could see white curtains in the windows and a fancy glass chandelier hanging from the rafters in the center. As his eyes surveyed the room he chuckled to himself thinking how out of place the restaurant seemed in such a remote part of the world. He noticed there were five tables scattered around in the room covered with clean white tablecloths. The restaurant was full except for one table that was located near a window that faced the street. A dark-skinned plump waitress who appeared to be French pointed Clede to the only vacant table. He sat down and she said, "What can I get for you, stranger," with a heavy accent.

As he started to ask her what was on the menu, a short golden-skinned man approached his table. Clede could tell he was Indian by the clothes and beads around his neck. The Indian and Clede's eyes met as the Indian spoke first with heavy broken English, "Min if'n I join ya? Al' ta ot'r places is'n tooken."

Clede looked him up and down then pushed an empty chair out with his boot. As the Indian sat down Clede spoke. "My name be Clede."

The Indian replied, "Thanks ma nam' Kiska. I cum down ta sell ma furs be headed north morrow. Ma people are ta Nootka's. Got um woman lil' cub. Goin' back 'fore winter build longhouse fer people."

Clede asked, "How far are your people from here?"

Kiska hesitated as he thought then answered, "Three er' fer moons travel fum 'ere."

Clede replied, "Would you care if I traveled with you? I need someone to show me how to get by in these parts. Maybe I could pay you in some way."

Kiska said, "We mak' um trade. I need 'elp wid longhouse. Mostly woman's and ole people in tribe, cud do with 'elp. Ya need 'elp to larn mountains. Much fine."

Clede replied, "I would be willing to do what I could if you let me winter over with your people?"

The Indian scratched his face and thought about it and then said, "We do gud tagether."

Then the waitress interrupted them as she read the menu out. Clede decided on fish and tators. Kiska said he would have the same. The waitress took their orders and then asked Clede, "What war you fight in, mister?"

Clede took a deep breath then spoke, "Is it your business, ma'am?"

The waitress just frowned then said, "No, guess not," as she turned and walked away.

Clede listened to Kiska's story of his family, home, and about the land and his only reason for coming into town was to trade his furs for things he couldn't get or make from the land. In the mountains, he said, the Great Spirit has his own set of rules that are much fairer then the white man's. They would travel many moons to reach his village. His words excited Clede. People were too complicated for him, the further he was away from civilization the better he would like it. Glory and fame was not a quest in his life. He had no use for gold other than to buy a few supplies. Kiska was a short squatty man of about five foot two with dark muscular arms and body. His dark, smooth silky skin made him look rather handsome in a hard way, but Clede knew that life had to have been difficult for him by the harshness he could see in his eyes. Clede believed he could trust this man but he wouldn't turn his back on him either. Kiska could show him a way of life that had existed among his people for thousands of years. Yep, he had a lot to learn before he would be ready to step out on his own.

The waitress interrupted his thoughts as she set their plates of food on the table. He was starving and with the smell of fresh-cooked fish he could hardly wait. They both nodded to her and Clede grabbed his fork and began to gulp the food down. The Indian watched him for a few moments then said, "Be'n long time no eat, eh?"

Clede didn't stop, just nodded his head and continued to eat. While he was eating, Clede told him about how he had come to be fighting for the past three years. He told Kiska about his wound and how it all saddened him. After they finished eating Clede spoke again saying, "I'll meet you at the trading post tomorrow before daylight. I would like to get a good night sleep before we head out." Kiska nodded in agreement, said he needed to trade for some things for his woman and child and he would see Clede in the morning. They must be leaving soon, sometimes an early snow could fall. They needed enough time to build the longhouse and be ready for the coming winter. Clede paid for their meals. They nodded as they both stepped out onto the wooden porch. He watched as the Indian headed for Bill's Trading Post and wondered what lay ahead.

Back on the street Clede squinted his eyes as he looked into the setting sun eyeing the hotel. His tired body and full stomach prompted him toward a quiet room and soft bed; he needed the rest, it had been a very long journey. The trip that lay ahead with the Indian would be another tough journey. Opening the door he entered Wilson's Hotel and walked up to the counter. A frail little man sat behind the counter. He wore a neatly pressed shirt, a vest and dark worn pants. The man asked, "What can I do for you, stranger?"

Clede replied, "Need a room for tonight only."

The man said, "Room three at the top of the stairs, first door on the right. That'll be two dollars in advance."

Clede dug into his pockets and brought out two dollars, paying the man. He picked up his bags and walked up the stairs. The price was outrageous but he was too tired to argue. He spotted the number three on the door to the right of the hall. He put the key in the lock and unlocked the door. The door creaked lightly as he swung it back and entered. There was a single bed under the window against the far wall, a shabby table with a pitcher of water, a bowl to put the water in and a small towel to wash his hands and face and dry off with. A single match lay close to the lamp. He lit the kerosene lamp, adjusted the brightness and sat down on the edge of the bed. Bending down he untied his army boots dropping them to the floor next to the bed. He stood up and stripped down to his underwear and flopped across the bed. The soft sheets and bed felt good against his weary traveled body. He better enjoy this, it might be a long time before he slept in a bed of this caliber. Picking himself up on his elbow he leaned over and blew out the lamp. Shadows from the activities down on the street danced on the ceiling over him. He could still hear people stirring on the street below as they noisily went about their business. As he lay there his mind drifted back to the battlefields, the sound of cannon fire, screaming men and the smells of death all around him. Slowly fatigue overtook him as he drifted into a tired, labored sleep.

The next morning he was awakened rudely by a loud noise out in the hall that caused him to jump to his feet. Startled he grabbed for his pistol that lay on the table. Not sure where he was for a moment. Jerking the door open he pointed his gun at the wide-eyed cleaning woman in the hall. She had dropped her cleaning bucket. With trembling lips she replied, "You're kinda jumpy, mister." Clede gave her a frown as he let the hammer down on his .44. He thought to himself, *You're lucky I look before I shoot.* A second glance revealed a rough-looking woman that was old way past her years. No doubt living here had been very hard for her. Even here she'd have a hard time to find a man who'd look at her twice.

Returning to his room he slammed the door behind him. He reached down and picked up his bag. Opening it he took out the buckskin pants and shirt he bought at the trading post. He'd heard enough about the war, he would leave his uniform in the room. Slipping a leg into the buckskin pants he put them on. Then he put on his shirt. He could still hear the cleaning woman in the hall, not as noisy now. Clede stood and bent over pouring water into the vase. Cupped the water in his hands and washed his face and hands, drying them on the single towel provided. Still fuming from being awakened he picked his pistol from the bed and shoved it into the scabbard. Then he buckled it loosely to his waist. His reflection in the window he shaped his mountain hat then screwed it down over his bushy red hair. Picked up his bag, leaving his uniform lying on the bed, he walked out.

Passing the counter he noticed the little man sleeping in his chair. He opened the door and stepped out onto the street. Hesitating for a few seconds to let his eyes adjust to the darkness. A light mist fell, the people still bustled around on the muddy street. He wondered if they ever slept. A faint glow on the horizon told him daylight would be breaking in an hour or so. As he approached the trading post he could see a light was glowing in the window. He hurriedly headed in that direction. As he entered the store he could see Kiska was already there. Kiska was standing near the counter talking to a tall, slim bearded man. As he came closer he could see the man shaking his fist in the Indian's face. Clede could tell by this scene that trouble was brewing for Kiska. Clede was a large man of about six foot four and weighed two hundred and forty pounds. As he came closer to Kiska and the man, he said, "You got everything, Kiska?"

The stranger and his size startled the bearded man. A puzzled look in his eye Clede could tell he wondered what this Nootka was to this stranger. Looking Clede up and down his stature seemed to intimidate this man. Then Kiska spoke, "Man no w'nt ta pa' me full price fer furs."

Clede turned with hard eyes and said, "It would be a good move on your part to deal fairly with my friend, mister."

The man glared at him for a moment but decided he needed help to deal with this buck-skinned stranger. Grudgingly he dug into his pocket and brought out several gold coins. He counted out the money and then stuffed it rudely into the Indian's hand. He turned and faced Clede. "You'er new around here. You best learn our ways."

Clede answering said, "And what ways would that be?" The man glared but said nothing as he turned and stomped out the door slamming the door behind himself.

Bill, the store owner, spoke, "That man is Mr. Wilson, he owns this town. He and his bullies don't take lightly to Indians, only want their business. He's been cheating them for as long as I can remember. You've made an enemy of the wrong man; he can be plenty of trouble in these parts. He's the law around here."

Clede answered Bill, "I'm looking for no trouble. I came to get my supplies and be on my way."

Bill went into the back and brought out their supplies and replied to Clede, "Watch yourselves leaving town. You have angered Wilson and he don't forget it."

Kiska had bought a pack mule from one of the miners who was down on his luck and needing money. He paid twice what the old broken-down animal was worth but they would need him to help carry the load of supplies. They loaded up the mule and then started slowly walking out of town toward the north. Bill stood at the door of the trading post and watched for a few seconds whispering under his breath, "Good luck." Then he turned and returned to his chores.

Clede walked behind the mule and Kiska took the lead. As they came to the end of the town three men stepped out into the street from behind the last tent. The shadows made it difficult at first to see the men's faces. One man about Clede's size with a big face full of beard and ugly as sin, the other two men stood back in the darkness. Clede didn't recognize any of them but he knew they meant trouble. The big man spoke first; he said, "Hey Injun, you owe my boss some money. You're not leaving until we get it."

The big man lowered his rifle and trained it on Kiska. They hadn't noticed Clede standing behind the rump of the mule. Clede slowly put his hand on his pistol, dropping his bag to the muddy street. Stepping out from behind the mule he faced the big man and spoke saying, "I don't know what you want, mister, but I figured we settled this argument back at the trading post. If your boss has a beef then it should be between him and the Indian."

The big man smiled. "I don't have any quarrel with you, only the Indian. But if you want some of the action that can be arranged." Staring at Clede and laughing he pulled the trigger on his rifle, the bullet catching Kiska in his left arm. Before the big man could pull his pistol Clede had his 44-caliber army pistol out and with lightning speed he fired a single round, dropping the big man with a slug between the eyes. Then cocking the hammer back quickly he turned and pointed it in the direction of the other two. They hadn't even had time to lift their weapons.

Clede stared with cold eyes at the two men and said, "More or do we end it here?"

The two men stood wide-eyed with cold fear running in their veins. They hadn't seen anyone in these parts handle a sidearm like this stranger. Slowly they bent over and grabbed the dead man by the feet. Backing down the street they kept their eyes on him till they were out of sight. Wilson's thugs out of sight, his attention quickly turned on Kiska. Clede whispered, "How bad you hit."

Kiska replied, "Only winged ma, I OK." Clede told him let's get out of here before they bring the whole gang. Grabbing the mule by the bridle Clede and Kiska moved quickly out of town. They traveled north, only stopping occasionally for Kiska to check his wound. Kiska led them across a couple of mountains before they felt safe enough to stop. Glancing back down the mountain looking for any motion like an eagle, looking at Clede he said, "I see no one follo'."

Clede noticed the blood dripping from his fingers and said, "You better tend to that wound."

Kiska walked into the forest and came back carrying a handful of leaves. He crushed them with a stone and mixed them with some water. He filled the wound with the contents and rapped his arm with a bandanna that Clede handed him. Kiska spoke, "I thin' I be OK. Glad u wid ma. Yar shoot much gud."

Clede replied, "I learned from my father. He was a lawman before he turned to farming. Besides, I've had a lot of practice.

After resting and treating the wound they pushed on, always looking back. They traveled all day, only stopping occasionally. As nightfall came they stopped to set up camp. Clede knew Kiska had lost some blood but even so he was tough to keep up with. Clede's bad leg ached him from the many miles they had traveled today. Pulling a leather strap from his bag on the mule he tied it tight around the calf muscle for support. It helped ease some of the pain. The Indian had some dried meat in his pack on the mule. He took a piece and threw the other piece to Clede. They both sat down on a log chewing on the jerky. They were a sight for sure, the Indian with a bloody arm and he with a bum leg. As he rubbed his leg the Indian spoke, "No mak'um fire ta nite. We mak'um shor no follo." Kiska laid out his Indian blanket, and then walked down to the bank of the little creek that trickled down off the mountain. Bending down he cupped some of the mud in his hands and covered his face and hands. He told Clede, "Ya do same. Many critters bite afta' dark." The mosquitoes were already buzzing around his head.

After applying the mud to his body he took off his black bear coat and lay it down. His army blanket he used to cover himself against the chill of the night. As he lay on his back looking into the night sky he could see what must have been millions of stars and occasionally a shooting star. In the distance he could hear the sound of a wolf singing his sad song, the gurgling sound of the creek as it made its way from the mountain on its way below. The peace, the smell of the trees, and the tranquility was exactly what he longed for. He felt remorse for having to kill the man back at Alki Point, but the way he looked at it, it was better him. He wouldn't venture back to Alki Point unless he was forced to.

Kiska whispered, "I take fi'st look. I wake nite." Clede nodded. They would have to make sure they weren't followed before there could be any relaxing. Pulling his army blanket up over his chest, his hat over his eyes, he closed his eyes and fell a sleep.

Somewhere around midnight Kiska kicked his boot for his watch. Clede picked up his rifle and made his way to where Kiska pointed. Clearing a place on the ground at the base of a tree he sat back and leaned against it. Clede pulled his coat up tight against his neck to keep the warmth in and the cold air out. A partial moon silhouetted the valley below and as he scanned the horizon for any sight of life he noticed a small lake in the distance. He could see the reflection of the moon and stars on it like a mirror. What a beautiful sight to behold. Squinting, he slowly strained his eyes but he could see no campfires in the valley below. Adjusted his pistol on his side and laid his rifle, a Kentuckian, across his lap.

As he sat there his memory returned to the loss of his mother and father back in Indiana. His folks were hardworking farmers who had migrated to America in search of a new life for themselves and their baby boy. Back in the old country his father had worked as a lawman, a job he didn't like because sometimes he would be forced to arrest friends. The job barely fed them, and after his father was shot they decided to move to the New World. The young couple sold all they owned and headed west. They were able to purchase a small farm in Indiana. The work was very hard but his father didn't mind—at least it was theirs. Clede grew up strong from the hard farming life but he never liked it. When the war broke out he was anxious to leave the farm for what he thought was going to be great adventure. His father became angry with him; after all, the entire farm would be his one day. Clede was his only child; his wife was unable to bear any more children. Besides, he told Clede, the war is not our affair. Clede's mind could not be changed and so one night he packed his few belongings and snuck off in the dark. A few months passed when Clede got the letter from the Joneses, who were good friends of the family. As he read the letter his heart burned from what he read, his parents had contracted smallpox and both perished. Mr. Jones went on to tell him in the letter that he buried them under the old tree that his mother and dad loved to rest under on Sunday. Several years would pass before he was able to return home. The farm was weathered and badly needing repair. He just was not a farmer, he had no desire to rebuild it. A broken-down farm and two graves under the tree, he wanted more. The Joneses gave him a good price for the old place. They agreed the spot where his parents were buried would be used as a burial place for their family. Free now to pursue his dream, there was nothing to hold him back and the money from the sale of the farm should be just about enough to get him where he wanted to go.

Suddenly Kiska touched his shoulder and pointed to the daylight breaking back in the east. That meant it was time to move. It would take some getting used to, the long summer days and short nights in the north. He had much to learn but there was no hurry now. As they sat eating some of the jerky in the darkness and waiting for enough daylight to travel, Kiska stood up and motioned for him to follow, and he grabbed his rifle and swung his backpack onto his back. Screwed down his hat and followed the mule and Kiska as they moved north again. He slipped through the woods like a snake slithering into his hole, not a sound or rolling of a stone, not even the cracking of a stick. They followed trails made by either animals or men, Clede wasn't sure which, at other times they followed a river or creek. The forest thickened and some places it almost blanked out the sun, but the Indian seemed to know his way easily through the forest. Clede was glad he met the Indian; he could just see himself out here lost in the dense forest going in circles for days. Kiska was using long years of experience.

Several hours passed as they came to a large range of mountains that were still snowcapped. Kiska stopped and pointed. He said, "O'er ot'er side be my village." Clede was feeling the strain of the quick pace they were traveling and was glad to hear they were near their destination. Little did he know it would take them close to two weeks to reach that mountain range.

They pushed on all that day but the mountains still seemed to be just as far away. They stopped to rest in a clearing, mostly for the mule's benefit, she was carrying the heavier load. Kiska walked out on the plateau of the mountain, scanned the terrain behind them for several minutes. He replied, "Tha no follo' us." That was welcome news to Clede's ears, he didn't want a shooting match with Wilson's thugs. He had enough killing to last him a lifetime.

They both sat down quietly to rest, Clede watched an eagle flying high overhead. Kiska moved back suddenly, motioning for Clede to freeze. Reaching into the backpack of the mule and untying his bow and taking two arrows from the sheave. Crouching down and slowly moving forward keeping a large boulder in front of him he crept up behind it then squatted down. Very slowly Clede leaned his head out so he could just see around the boulder. There he saw what Kiska was looking at. A very large mule deer with head down was pawing and eating at a patch of grass. The deer didn't notice them because they hid behind the boulder. When Kiska was within about twenty yards of the deer he cocked his bow, aimed, and then slowly let the bowstring slip from his fingers. The arrow made a hissing sound as it cut through the forest air with great speed toward its mark. Clede watched as the arrow struck the large animal just behind its ear. The deer never knew what hit him; he dropped, kicking a few times, and then went limp. Clede was amazed at the skill this Indian had using such a primitive weapon. Kiska loaded his remaining arrow into the bow as he came to his feet and approached the lifeless deer. Clede watched as Kiska circled the deer, coming up behind the fallen animal. He kicked the rump of the deer with his moccasins. The deer showed no signs of life. It was a buck with a large rack of antlers. Dropping down to his knees he raised his hands to the sky and chanted. He was thanking the Great Spirit for this gift. After his prayer Kiska took his knife from his scabbard and with the precision of a surgeon gutted the deer. The Indian ate some of the raw liver. Offered some to Clede but he declined, he preferred his cooked.

Together they dragged the animal back up the mountain to where the mule was tied. Kiska removed a hindquarter, leaving the leg to tie it to the mule. Kiska spoke saying, "We ned 'fore git ta ma tribe." After washing up and cleaning his hands and knife they broke camp. Kiska took the rein of the mule and motioned for Clede to follow. They moved on, crossing the valley and up the mountains that he had seen a week before. The magnitude of this land was mind-boggling, what a sight. A river wound its way between the mountains heading for the sea somewhere in the far distance. The water was crystal clear as all the waters were. The water looked inviting for a swim but they must push on, time was important. They stopped just for a minute and Clede glanced back visualizing in his mind a log cabin.

Several hours passed when Kiska motioned for him that this would be where they would set up camp. They had been following a creek that branched off from the river. They both went down to the stream's edge and washed and drank their fill of the ice-cold water. As Clede drank from the stream he saw several fish lazily swimming in the depths below. Kiska said, "Tanite' we at' much gud. Yo' start fire." Clede gathered up wood and Kiska showed him how to start a fire his way. Today he learned his first rule of how to start a fire. Kiska replied, "I sho' yo' fire." A straight stick, a piece of leather strap and a flat chunk of bark, he sat down and worked the stick back and forth, adding dry grass till a stream of smoke materialized. Bending over, Kiska blew on them until a flame leaped into sight. Adding larger kindling they soon had a nice campfire blazing. Trimming two branches with his knife into a sharp point he stuck the pieces of meat on the ends of the sticks. Angling them across the fire they would soon be eating the venison. After tending to the mule's needs and laying the camp out they both relaxed checking the venison from time to time. The cooked meat was a delightful change from what they ate on the trail. As they sat savoring the cooked meat Clede could hear the sound of loons in the distance; he knew they were in the river that the little creek emptied into. The quiet sound of the stream flowing through the forest sang a song to his ears. An owl hooted somewhere back in the forest as he readied himself for a nighttime hunt. Kiska spoke, "We follo' wata thro' mountain. No sno' thar. Much easy walk'."

Clede watched as Kiska covered himself with mud and he did likewise. Clede's body was sore but each day he could feel his body getting stronger and stronger. He poured some water on his bandana from a water bag and then rubbed his sore feet and calf muscle with the cool water. The water felt good. Kiska would take the first watch; he knew that Clede needed rest more than he did. His arm was healing nicely, the herbs from the leaves were doing the job. Clede put his boots back on and lay out his bed. Rifle beside him, he lay his pistol on his stomach and fell asleep.

Chapter 2

Early the next morning he awakened suddenly when he felt a hand over his mouth. As his eyes cleared it was Kiska pointing toward the river. Coming to a sitting position he saw what Kiska was pointing at—three men in a canoe paddling downstream. Kiska whispered, "No tell men gud er bad, better be safe, cum." Quickly Clede strapped on his pistol and followed Kiska into the cover of the forest. In their haste to conceal themselves they had forgotten to extinguish the campfire. Clede's eyes met Kiska's as they watched the small stream of smoke drift up through the forest. They could only hope that the men would be self-occupied enough to miss spotting the smoke.

Clede studied the three men as they came nearer. He noticed from their dress and skin color that they appeared to be French. Luck was not with them today, however; one of the men eyed the smoke from the front of the canoe. Pointing his finger toward the campfire they turned their canoe toward the shore, the two men in the front picked up their rifles as the man in the rear paddled the boat to the edge of the bank. Clede and Kiska watched as the men with weapons ready stepped out of the canoe, pulling it up on the riverbank. Clede had made a stupid mistake not to grab his rifle leaning against the tree where he had lain. Checking his pistol he had at least six shots—he would have to make them count if he needed them. Several yards away he could see that Kiska only had his knife. The three men definitely had them outnumbered and outgunned. Clede thought, he hoped these three came in peace but by the looks of them he was hoping for too much.

The mule was tied to a tree twenty feet from the campfire near the heavy tree line. The old mule wasn't interested in the events unfolding, she was more interested in the clump of grass at the base of the large fir tree. The two men who had been in the front of the canoe walked up the riverbank and cautiously approached the smoldering fire. The third man squatted down next to the front of the canoe. With rifles ready for action the two near the fire cautiously scanned the area of the camp looking for whose fire this was. The man who appeared to be the leader wore a green sock hat with buckskin jacket and pants. He motioned to the man behind him to go check the mule. Clede caught sight of Kiska hiding behind a large fir tree near where the mule was tied. Gesturing with his hands Clede knew that Kiska was telling him they wanted the supplies strapped to the mule. They couldn't let them have their supplies, they needed them for themselves. Clede checked but his powder and balls were in the pack on the mule. If there was going to be a fight he hoped they could end it quickly. Glancing back again toward Kiska, to his surprise, the Indian had disappeared. A sudden feeling of fear came over him as he figured the Indian had run out on him. But there was no time for him to think about that now; he couldn't let them have those supplies. Without them would be sure death.

Clede couldn't move without revealing his location, he would have to bide his time. Six shots and surprise was all he had going for him. Those rifles sure had the range on him and he didn't want any part of a hot slug. His leg ached from the last slug he took. *I have to work my way into range so I at least have a fighting chance with this pistol,* he thought. He heard the man near the mule shout, "Look at the markings on this blanket, Pierre. Those belong to a Nootka."

This was his chance, and perhaps his only chance to make a move. The Frenchmen, for the moment, were preoccupied with the mule; he slowly began to work his way through the trees. Jumping from one tree then to the next one, being careful not to be seen by the one squatting on the ground next to the canoe. For now his eyes were on his buddies as they investigated the mule. Finally he figured he was in range. He checked his position; here he would be shielded from the man at the canoe. That would make the odds two to one for the moment. This was the best opportunity to make his stand. Taking a deep breath to steady his nerves he stepped from behind the tree where he hid and with a loud voice, so no doubt he would be heard, Clede replied, "You fellars like my mule and supplies, do you?"

The two men jumped with surprise at the sound of another human being speaking in English and so close to them. Where did this white man come from?—they were expecting a lone Indian. The one with the stocking hat spun around and fired his rifle at Clede, hitting the tree above his head. Clede fired his pistol with lightning speed and with a loud bang the smoke belched from his pistol. The bullet found its mark, hitting the man in the chest. He groaned as blood soaked the front of his buckskin shirt. He collapsed to the ground and lay motionless. Clede fired another round but missed as the other Frenchman dove in behind the trees. Taking a quick glance around the tree toward the canoe, the man had disappeared. They had him pinned down and in only a matter of a few seconds would have him in crossfire. He heard a shot and saw the mule fall dead. One of them had shot the mule. His mind raced with thoughts of what his next move would be, then he caught movement at the corner of his eye. Kiska was sneaking in behind the man hiding near the mule. He sure felt better about the Indian now. His outcome to this situation was improving. The Frenchmen didn't realize there were two of them. They figured Clede was the only one they had to be concerned with. They had him where they wanted, now to finish him off. Kiska behind a tree behind the man raised the knife and threw it. There was a dull thud and groan from the Frenchman as the knife stuck to the hilt in the back of his head. He slowly sank to the ground, falling against a tree. The third man, near the canoe, ran and pushed it into the river. He fired a shot toward Clede but the bullet went far right, hitting a tree. Paddling wildly his canoe caught the flow and he slipped out of sight down the river. Clede turned and yelled to Kiska, "I guess he didn't like the odds." They both laughed with relief that the ordeal was over and they were still breathing to see another day.

Clede and Kiska checked the two dead men to make sure they weren't playing possum. Clede then said to Kiska with a big grin on his face, "We make a good team. I guess we better bury these two." Clede bent down and picked up the rifle lying near the lifeless body of the one called Pierre. "He won't need this anymore," he replied. Examining the rifle, it was a 50-caliber Hawkens, a much better rifle than the Kentuckian he bought back at Alki Point. This rifle, although shorter in barrel length than the Kentuckian, was 50-caliber and used percussion caps. He had tried to buy one back in Alki Point but with the gold rush Bill was sold out. The larger caliber would give him the extra knockdown power he needed for larger game. He took Pierre's bag that contained the caps and balls. He had learned a lesson—from now on he would keep his rifle close at hand. Killing again left a bad taste in his mouth but self-preservation was what he had to do. It seemed the more he ran from trouble the more it hunted him down.

Looking at Kiska, Clede asked him if he'd ever seen these men before. Kiska shook his head, no. He said, "Many c'me h're fo' differ'nt reasons. Most c'me lookin' fer gold er furs."

Clede replied, "Men down on their luck will do some crazy things. I think they figured it would be an easy steal." Kiska bent down and cut the leather halter that held the pack to the mule. Pulling it from under the dead animal he separated their gear. Clede gathered up his part. Kiska sliced some of the meat from the mule; they would eat this until they made a fresh kill. He said, "We et' this later. Not have ta hunt, only trav'l." Clede didn't cherish eating mule but he knew that Kiska was right. They knew the extra load would slow them down but they would need all of it. Clede and Kiska would miss the old mule—the extra weight meant much tougher going. Kiska made a travois so he could drag rather than carry his load. Clede, being a much larger man than Kiska, could carry his part on his back. He cut two limbs from a tree nearby and fashioned them to his backpack so he could support the extra load. No matter the difficulty, he had to have this gear some now, the rest he would use later when he set out on his own.

They buried the two men and tried to conceal the campsite as though no one had ever been there. That way if the Frenchman brought help back with him it would be harder for them to pick up their trail. They spent most of the day burying the two dead men. The graves had to be deep enough to keep animals from digging them back up. Kiska and Clede drug the remainder of the mule they cut in pieces down to the river and dumped it in. Some of the body parts sank and some flowed downstream. They would spend one more night near the river but not in this same location. They would move upriver and this time no fires. They would take turns watching the river in case more unsuspecting visitors decided to drop in on them. This land could be unforgiving and many who came to hunt for the yellow metal or furs found only an early grave. The further they traveled north the less chance for seeing white men. He yearned for this life—it could be hard but it made more sense than war. With the help of this Indian friend he would learn the rules in this part of the world.

At daybreak they hit the trail again as soon as they had enough light to see. Kiska took the lead, as they were interested in putting some distance from this location. They traveled through the saddle in the mountain just as Kiska had promised they would several weeks back. The extra weight of the backpack slowed them down considerably. Several hours of following the river they stopped to rest and Clede took the time to readjust the backpack. The leather straps cut into his shoulders and with Kiska's help he added some extra padding. They sure did miss that old flop-eared mule. Clede felt bad about whipping her at times to get her to move. Even with this added weight his body was slowly strengthening to the point he could actually enjoy a day's march. Kiska was right, the higher elevations still had plenty of snow up there. Bending down he scooped up some of the snow and also rubbed the white stuff over his face, eating some of it. The snow tasted good to his dry mouth, it was tough going. Kiska motioned to Clede and he lifted himself up with the help of his rifle for support. He adjusted the backpack for the most comfort, then they moved on. They crossed several mountains, always keeping the river within sight. Kiska pushed hard. Clede could tell he was anxious to get home. Each day as night fell they would collapse in exhaustion, barely capable of setting up camp before dropping off to sleep. Clede looked forward to rest and a warm meal at the end of the day. The mule wasn't the best he'd ever eaten but he didn't mind.

They'd been on the trail for about six weeks since their quick departure from Alki Point and the nasty incident with Wilson's thugs. Just about two weeks since the trouble with the Frenchmen. Still they would look back occasionally just to make sure someone wasn't following them. Clede wasn't sure what month they were in—maybe it was May or June, guessing by the looks of the season.

One evening as Clede followed behind Kiska, keeping his thoughts off the weight of his pack, suddenly he noticed a fork in the river. Kiska looked at Clede and he noticed a change in his facial expression that told him this was a place he knew well. Kiska picked up the pace to almost a trot. Clede was finding it more and more difficult to keep up with the Indian. They followed the fork that branched off to the northeast. As they followed the riverbank Clede spotted a small curl of smoke lazily drifting up through the trees just upriver. Kiska startled him when he gave out with a call like an owl. In the distance near the direction of the smoke came a like response. Through the trees he spotted a small line of makeshift huts just at the edge of the forest back from the river. As they came closer to the village Kiska dropped his travois and spoke something in his native language to the group.

A short pudgy dark woman with long braided hair and wearing clothes of decorated buckskin ran toward them. As she came closer she was mumbling something in Noot and jumped into Kiska's arms, knocking him back. Clede grinned—he knew this funny little squatty woman was Kiska's woman. Kiska gently put his hand over her mouth and said something that quieted her down. He then faced the tribe of the village and pointed at Clede, speaking first in his language then in his broken English. "This ma gud frien'. Save ma lif' back on trail."

The woman walked over to Clede and hugged him, muttering in Noot to him. He smiled and nodded his head in agreement to whatever it was that she said. Kiska introduced her as Tenakee. Clede pointed a finger at himself and said, "Clede." The woman made a try at pronouncing his name but the best she could do was "Cleke."

The village consisted of about five or six families living in small huts huddled close together. The men excitedly helped Kiska unload his travois. The supplies he brought would make life much easier for all of them. Kiska and Clede followed Tenakee into a small hut as the rest of the tribe returned to their daily chores. Clede bent over to enter the hut and once inside stood for a few seconds to allow his eyes to adjust to the darkness. Inside was a small boy of about two years old and Kiska laughed and picked him up tickling him and talking to him in Noot. Clede knew this must be li'l cub and Kiska called him "Keenah." The boy laughed and smiled with delight at seeing his father again. Clede could see that his friend had a fine family and a great place to raise him. The boy laughed and giggled with delight in seeing his father again. He wondered how long these people would be able to live in peace before the wave of immigrants overtook them. They sat eating fish and berries as Clede listened to the talking with Kiska every now and then interpreting.

Clede sat resting near the fire that burned in the center of the village. He could see three canoes pulled up on the bank in the distance by the river. The Nootkas were very skillful builders and decorators of canoes. Each canoe was decorated with designs that told a story about the builder of the canoe. Kiska explained this to him later. Their primary food supply came from the waterways but they also would hunt in the forest. The land was rich with game and an abundance of waterways made life much easier for the Indians of the Northwest compared to other tribes of North America. The Noots even hunted in the Pacific, even killing whales on occasion. In the center of the village stood a tall totem pole that had been skillfully crafted depicting the clan status, spirits, and stories of significance. They could stand as high as forty feet.

Clede noticed a woman bathing her baby in the river. He decided that was a good idea and about time he done the same. He told Kiska of his plans and Kiska told him there was a deeper hole in the curve of the river just upstream from the village. Grabbing his rifle he traveled upstream, following the river till he came to the curve that Kiska spoke of. A hole had been dug in the opposite bank by the river. The water was very clear he could see small fish swimming near the center of the river. Setting his rifle against a large boulder he unbuckled his pistol and laid it next to his rifle. He stripped down naked and waded into the frigid waters, stopping once to adjust to the cold. He glanced around once to make sure no one was watching him. Wading out until the water was waist deep he started to bathe himself. He shivered as the slow moving waters cupped around his bare body. He dove under and swam out to the pocket then back to where his feet touched the rocky bottom. The water felt good on his sore shoulders from carrying the heavy backpack. Retrieving his clothes he washed them then laid them out on the rocks to dry. He lay down next to his clothes and enjoyed the warm sun that dried him. Falling off to sleep he thought about their journeys and where he would go from here.

Later that evening after his refreshing bath and a nice nap he rejoined the tribe. The clean clothes, the nap, and refreshing bath gave him an appetite, he was ready to eat. Tenakee and other women of the village had cooked a meal of fish and some kind of mush they mixed up. She offered some of it to him. He took some of the fish and a small wooden bowl of the mush. Clede didn't dare ask what was in the mush, he figured he was better off not asking. He dipped his fingers into the mush and carefully tasted it with his tongue. The taste was strong and not favorable to his liking but he maintained his facial expression so as not to hurt her feelings. He managed to swallow a little of it as Tenakee looked on. The fish was a different story, however. Looking at Tenakee he rubbed his stomach in approval. The woman nodded, grinning and saying something in Noot, then she returned to her cooking chores. As he sat eating he studied the Noots carefully, watching them go about their daily duties. He noticed a parallel between them and his folks back home. The customs, dress and way of doing things were somewhat different but just the same they were a warm, loving people. Only aim in life was to raise a family and live in peace. Watching them brought back memories of his father and mother and he missed them. Yep, there had been some good times; he felt sorry that his father and he didn't see eye to eye. They were gone now and life was moving in a different direction for him, just memories now. The brightly colored patterns of the Indian artwork were beautiful and fascinating to behold. Their way of life was simple and easy, much different than the work back on his father's farm. This was a paradise with their livelihood there for the taking. Each of the individuals down to the smallest child had a purpose and a place in their daily life. The children worked hard but they didn't seem to mind because they knew their duties were important to the well-being of the tribe. There was a great closeness and family atmosphere. Kiska sat down and told him of wars with other tribes but he said seldom was there bloodshed. Then he asked Clede, "Arn ya rested?" Clede nodded his head. Kiska replied, "Gud ta morra we start warkin' on longhouse. Winta cum fast be ready fer many cold days." If they hurried and winter didn't come early, they should have enough time to finish the longhouse before the first hard snow. The two men parted, as Clede knew he needed rest and would need his strength to help build the longhouse tomorrow. As he opened the flap to his hut he heard and noticed a line of geese as they flew high overhead. Watching them for a few seconds he closed the flap of his hut and retired for the day.

Clede wintered with the Nootkas his first year in the Northwest. He lived up to his part of the bargain and learned a lot and taught some of his building skills to the Noots. The hut the women and old folks had constructed for him proved to be much more than adequate for him. The longhouse was fashioned into a large rectangle and a wall was built to create a separate room at the back of the long building. This separate room was set aside for the chief and his family. Kiska was the chief and this room would be for him and his family exclusively. The oldest man of the group, named Nayuki, supervised the particular construction of this room. It took them, with the help of Clede, several days to finish this part of the building. The whole tribe was on hand to catch the expression of Kiska as he and his family prepared to move in. Even though the proud chief tried not to show emotion it was apparent how proud he was. The Nootkas had a chain of command that was nearly sacred. Each member and family would take their places along the long wall on each side of the longhouse. The least significant of the tribe always were nearest to the doorway. A large fire was to be kept burning in the center of the building at all times. It was the responsibility of the women and children to see that the fire remained burning. A stack of wood must be replenished periodically so as to have plenty of wood for the fire.

The large timbers that were used for the construction were fashioned much in the same manner as the pioneers built their log buildings. Straw and mud were mixed together and stuffed into the cracks between the logs to keep the cold air from penetrating the room. A large hole in the roof of the longhouse allowed the smoke a means for escaping. During snowstorms and blizzards a flap could be pulled over the hole to shut out the storm. The younger men of the village were to hunt and catch fish to keep the tribe well-fed. They built traps in the river to corner the fish thus making it easier to spear them. The longhouse must be stocked and everyone was busy at work. The first light snow had already fallen when a cold front blew in from the north. The stench of fish was strong in the village as it hung to dry.

The longhouse was finally completed other than the décor that would be painted to the front. The storeroom was fully stocked and the little village was ready now for the coming winter. Those who worked hard in building the structure could now spend their time on fishing and hunting. The women would tidy up the longhouse and go about setting things in order, as women will do. The huts were torn down and the material was used where possible for the longhouse. Some of the remainder that couldn't be used would be burned in the fire for firewood.

Kiska, Clede and a couple of the older men spent their time working on a smaller building which would be attached to the side of the longhouse. This building when constructed would be used as a storehouse for food supplies. A small doorway was cut in the wall so that the longhouse and storage building could be accessed. This doorway was cut small so that a person could just pass into the storage room. A deerskin was hung to close this passage. The reason behind the skin would be to keep the warmth from the longhouse from entering the storage room. All the cracks in both buildings were filled in and the structures were sealed to keep the small animals from creeping in to steal food.

The women made baskets from reeds they found along the river edge. The children searched the forests for berries that would fill those baskets. The women went to great strides in making the baskets and decorating them. The village reminded Clede of an ant mound as he watched all doing their part.

Clede made many friends in the Nootka village. He managed to learn some of the Noot language, which delighted them. Clede paid close attention to learn all that would be possible in the time he would spend with these people. On days when the weather was bad and most stayed indoors he would watch the women sewing and making buckskin clothing for their families. He learned how to make spears, bow and arrows for shooting fish and game.

The days shortened as they moved into late fall and their first good snowfall lay on the ground turning everything into a clean beautiful white. During the day Clede would join the men of the tribe who sat around the fire in the center of the building. The fire was kept burning and plenty of dry wood for the fire must be stacked up. The children would go in pairs out to gather wood for safety. The smoke hung like a New England fog inside the building with some filtering out through the small hole in the roof.

Chewing on a piece of dried elk meat he wiped the tears from his eyes caused by the heavy smoke. He snickered as he watched Malakaya organizing and giving orders like a military general. She was responsible for the well-being and running the business of the village. Her authority was only second to the chief himself. All the meals, fire, and firewood plus organizing the work groups to take care of whatever would be needed for the village to run smoothly. The older of the younger men was in charge of the daily hunting and fishing expeditions if needed. Kiska, the chief, his responsibility was for overlooking the protection of the tribe plus organizing hunts. But all was not work, there were times of games and relaxation for all. The men sat near the fire telling stories as the young men and boys listening intently. Clede had to tell his story again about how he and Kiska outsmarted the gang in Alki Point. He would draw his pistol and point it as if shooting the big man. They would all clap and laugh with enjoyment begging him to tell the story again. Clede noticed a couple of the young women of the tribe smiling at him. Kiska leaned against him and whispered they were looking for a husband. Clede was glad it was dark so that Kiska wouldn't see him blush. He had plans but they didn't include a wife.

A sentry was always posted in a locale that could watch over the village for any who might come to war against them. Clede, as an accepted member of the tribe, was expected to take his turn on watch. A duty that he enjoyed because it gave him time to be alone and think. As a young soldier he had done his share of sentry duty. A mountain rose up behind the village that they would climb to set their watches. From this vantage point you could see well down and up the river plus he could see the village below. Seldom was the tribe attacked but there had been a few instances in the past. Mostly the skirmishes consisted of stealing from one another rather than leading to bloodshed. As he sat watching over the village below he thought how wrong the white man's assessment was of these people. He could not find a big difference in both peoples except for language and culture. He noticed the death of a member of the Nootkas was a very tragic event but accepted part of their life. They prayed and thanked the Great Spirit for everything they had. Yes, they were a very humble people just trying to live out their lives in peace in this raw, untamed part of the world.

When old man winter came it was with a vengeance. The cold blustery wind blew across the little village with a blinding snowstorm. The little beaver-dammed lake began to freeze over. The high winds piled snow up against the outside of the longhouse, but it was warm and snug inside, as the Nootkas had prepared well. Their many hours of hard work were paying off; they would be safe from what the winter had to bring them.

The days passed and they entered into the deep part of the long cold winter. Clede listened as the winds blew outside. He thought about the winters back on the farm. They received a lot of snow, most of it coming off the Great Lakes. Those winters could be hard back there, just depending on how well the farm prospered that year. He remembered on one occasion, when he was very young, his father had gone out in a blizzard much the same as this one to hunt for food. He remembered they thought they lost him but he managed to crawl back to the cabin. The frostbite on his toes caused him to lose his little toe on his right foot. How afraid he was that his dad had perished in the storm. A real stroke of luck, his meeting Kiska. Imagine himself out in this storm and cold trying to survive till the weather broke. He would remember as he traveled to stop and build himself a shelter maybe not as elaborate as the longhouse but a place to hold up till the hard part of winter passed. His thoughts were interrupted as Kiska sat down next to him. He showed him how to construct eyewear to protect his eyes from snow blindness. Snow blindness could be fatal to a man traveling alone. Unbeknownst to Clede, the many things he would learn this year living with the Noots would save his life many times in the future.

Some of the Noots spent time tattooing their bodies. They did this for many reasons, such as warding off evil spirits, a way to identify an individual should he be mutilated in battle, or maybe just to beautify themselves to attract the opposite sex. In any case Clede felt no inclination to tattoo himself as the Nootkas did. The shaman or witch doctor's responsibility was to protect the individuals of the tribe against evil spirits.

Several weeks passed and signs of the end of winter began to appear. The storms were less frequent and violent than they had been in the dead of winter. The days began to be longer and there were times to venture out and hunt for fresh meat. The ice began to melt and the waterways ran quickly from the snowmelt. With the approaching of summer Clede became more restless and Kiska could sense his friend was anxious to be moving on. He felt that he had come a long way and was ready to try out his skill on his own. Kiska would have him stay and marry one of the available squaws but he knew his dreams and heart were somewhere else across the mountains.

One day as the sun broke across the mountains east of the village, Clede knew the time had come. He spent several hours carefully packing his backpack. Tenakee brought him much dried meat to take on his journey. It would hold him over and give him many days' journey before he would have to hunt. She packed a leather bag made from the stomach of a deer with berries. Soon he was ready and as he stepped through the doorway of the longhouse the whole village was there to say good-bye. Clede approached Kiska and held out his Kentuckian rifle with a scabbard that he worked on during the winter. The Indian gave him a big smile and thanked him for such a gracious gift. Kiska handed him a large knife in a sheath decorated with the Nootka art colors. The two men stood looking at each other and Kiska replied, "Yo cum long journey, ma frien'."

Clede then spoke, "You always be my friend. Until we meet again." They hugged and then Clede turned and followed the river upstream. As he reached a knoll he turned back and gave out with his best owl imitation. With delight he heard many villagers reply in like manner. He lifted his arm high and stepped off the knoll out of sight. This closed the chapter on a part of his life he would not forget, nor his good friends the Nootkas.

Chapter 3

Clede, who was following the river, changed his direction and climbed up the side of a mountain. Stopping for a second to catch his breath he looked back and could see a thin stream of smoke in the far distance. It was coming from the Nootkas' village; this would be the last he would see them. For just a moment he felt very alone, he would miss his good friend Kiska and his people. There was something across the next mountain that he must see. With his Hawkens in his right hand he moved on across this mountain and another before he would stop again. He remembered Kiska's advice—he would travel slow, quietly and always being aware that he could become the hunted. Moving north he lost sight of the river but as he dropped off the second mountain and walked into the valley he saw a small creek winding down from the mountain. A snowmelt creek lazily wound its way across the valley. He could hear the bubbling sound as it echoed through the forest trees. A dead log near the creek would be a good place to stop and rest for a while. He set his rifle against the log and dropped his backpack. Stooping over he took out some of the dried meat that Tenakee had packed for him. Clearing a spot on the ground next to the log he sat down and began eating the meat. The meat tasted good and he chuckled to think about the funny little woman called Tenakee. Kiska's many warnings came to his mind as he watched the weather. He kept his rifle close at hand and his eyes were always moving, scanning, looking for movement of any kind. After finishing the jerky he grabbed his rifle and walked to the creek. Bending down he cupped some of the very cold water and drank his fill. Lifting himself up using his rifle for support he returned to pick up his backpack and moved north once again. The mountain before him was very steep; he would go around the mountain rather than over it. He could see the top was capped very heavily with a deep powder of snow. He had no desire to try and trek through the snow, he wasn't in any hurry.

As late evening started to fall he spotted a flat piece of ground where a small trickle of a creek made its way along an embankment. This looked like a good place for camp. The water in the creek was clear and very cold and he would be hidden from anyone above. He could see a good view below also. Resting his knee on the ground at the edge of the creek he bent over and cupped some of the water in his palm. His eyes scanned his surroundings for any unexpected danger that might be near. Out of the corner of his eyes he caught a movement in the waters. A small trout swam lazily heading downstream with the current flow. Then he noticed another and another—there were several in and around the rocks at the bottom of the creek. He thought they were looking for a bug or anything falling into the water that was edible. Then he remembered the bow and arrow that Kiska helped him make back at the Nootkas' village during the winter. A couple of trout roasted over a fire would sure taste better than the dried meat in his backpack. Backing away from the creek slowly he unhooked his backpack and dropped it to the ground then laid his rifle across it. He took the bow from around his body and two arrows from his pack. One of the arrows he put in his teeth, the other he loaded into the bow. Crouching low so his shadow wouldn't cast shadows on the creek he slowly approached the creek where he had spotted the trout. Squatting down on his knees he watched in the water for movement. A few minutes passed as he watched motionless, then he saw a large trout swim out from under a rock. Patiently he waited till the fish turned his side toward Clede before he attempted a shot. Kiska's words came back to always be patient to wait for your best opportunities for a kill. Slowly he pulled the arrow back to his cheek, breathed out, took careful aim and let the arrow slip from his fingers. The arrow swished as it leaped from the bow making a small splash as it entered the water. He had aimed just below the fish to allow for the rising of the arrow. The fish leaped as the arrow went over him; he swam quickly downstream and out of sight. Clede cursed to himself for missing such an easy shot. He'd try again—there was still awhile before darkness. Bending over, he fished the floating arrow from the creek and laid it on the ground next to him. He took the one from his teeth and reloaded the bow.

Several minutes passed before the stream settled down and fish began to return to norm. Another one came in range, this time he would take better aim. Holding his breath he let the arrow fly and this time the arrow hit its target, catching the fish behind the gills. Blood darkened the water, dropping his bow he pulled at the leather strap attached to the arrow. A nice catch, he thought to himself, as he pulled the wiggling trout from the creek. This was a very nice fish, no need for him to get another. He held the fish down with his left hand and took his knife from his side. Scaling and gutting the fish he threw the remains back into the water. They would make a great feast for the other trout. Wiping his knife on his pants he washed the fish in the creek then picked up his bow and arrows and returned to his campsite. He whittled out a small spear from a tree branch and shoved it through the mouth and into the tail section of the fish. Quickly he started a fire and piled rocks in a ring, positioning the fish over the flames. Satisfied dinner would soon be cooked he gathered up enough dead wood to hold him over through the night. He stopped to adjust the fish several times to make sure it was cooked on all sides. As the fish continued to cook he finished putting his campsite in order. Then he sat down, crossing his legs near the fire, checking the cooking fish. Once satisfied it was cooked he pulled some of the meat from the fish and ate. The hot food tasted good—he hadn't had a cooked meal since he left the village. He surveyed his position as he ate and was satisfied he was well protected on all sides from surprise. The mush cakes the squaws packed would be dropped along the trail for any critter that could stomach them. He ate the entire fish till there was just a small pile of bones next to the fire.

His travels had brought him a long way that day and the warm food left him feeling sleepy. Darkness had come in and around the forest. He got up and walked over to the creek. Drinking his fill of the water he scraped some of the mud from the side of the bank and covered his hands and face. Back at the fire he laid another large log on the fire and made himself a bed near it. Using the blanket from the Noots he laid that on the ground and used his coat to cover himself. As he lay there staring into the flickering fire his mind wondered back to one of the young girls who had become interested in him. She couldn't have been more than fourteen or fifteen years old, but they were ready for a man by that age. Nice catch for a man interested in a wife, but not him. These Indian girls were a lot tougher than those he remembered back in Indiana. Life had been very hard for his father and mother. His father just wasn't cut out to be a farmer, but he tried. He thought Mom had been really glad when his father had quit his job as a deputy and they had decided to go west to America. He wondered could it have been the smallpox or did they just work themselves to death. Getting up on one arm he threw one more piece of wood on the fire then checked his rifle next to his side. Laying his pistol on his chest he pulled his hat down over his eyes and drifted off to sleep.

Sometime early in the morning before daylight he was awakened by the sound of rocks rattling along the shore of the creek. He lay silently listening to the sound that appeared to be about twenty yards downstream. Glancing into the night sky he figured it must be two or three hours before daylight. His fire had nearly gone out, only a few dimly glowing coals was all that remained. He decided the best course of action was to lie there silently. Perhaps it was just some small animal searching for something to eat along the creek bank. Reaching in the dark he located his rifle near his side. He sat up and strapped his pistol scabbard on pushing the pistol into it. Then he eased the hammer back on his Hawkens making sure not to let it make a sound. With his left hand he slowly slid his fur coat off his legs. The smell of smoke hung heavily in the camp from the few embers that remained. Scooting back he rested his back against the tree and laid his rifle across his lap. Another stone rattled, this time much closer than before. His heart began to pound heavy as his eyes strained to see anything in the very dim light. Then in the darkness he saw the reflection of two large yellow eyes. It was so close he could hear the heavy steady breathing from the creature's nostrils. Filled with fear he knew it must be a large bear by the size and distance between the eyes that glowed back at him. Slowly he lifted his rifle from off his legs and pointed it in the direction of the animal. The beast probably caught scent of the fire and leftover fish from his meal last night. As it came closer he placed a sweaty finger over the trigger and slowly squeezed it. There was a loud report and blinding flash as the Hawkens bellowed in the darkness. The deafening sound broke the stillness as the sound echoed through the forests. Laying his rifle across his lap he jerked the pistol from its scabbard on his side. A few seconds passed as he strained his ears for any sound in the dark. Then he heard a mournful growl just ten feet from where he sat. He saw the large creature as it rolled across the hot coals in an attempt to regain its feet. In the dim light he fired at the silhouette three times, quickly firing and refiring his pistol, he listened and looked for any sign of the beast. Coming to his feet he struggled in the dark to find his powder horn and caps to reload the rifle. Finding his powder horn and grabbing it with his right hand he attempted to reload in the dark. Then he heard a loud crash some distance back in the forest. He could tell the bear was hurt badly as he stumbled to get away. Then quiet returned as the only sound he could hear was his heavy breathing.

Once his rifle was loaded he gathered the coals together and soon had a roaring fire going. He returned to sit down by the tree and reloaded his pistol also. That done he sat quietly listening for any sound of the great creature he had just encountered. His eyes scanned the perimeter of the firelight but he could see nothing. Once again familiar sounds of the bubbling creek and an occasional owl could be heard through the forest. Moving out close to the campfire he lay down near the fire with his rifle in hand. He would try and get some sleep before daylight then figure out what happened last night.

Clede sat up and pulled some of the dried meat from his pack as he stroked the fire. He noticed a lone hawk flying overhead as it circled on the hunt for breakfast. With enough light now he surveyed the campsite and could see the signs of what happened in the darkness. By the prints he could tell it was a large bear, probably a grizzly or brown bear by the size of the tracks. There was a large pile of fur mixed with blood near the edge of the camp and he could see the animal was hit well by the large drops of blood. He felt damn lucky that he was still breathing; the animal had come within ten feet of where he lay by the tree. Next time he would be more careful to cover up the remains of the fish. Clede walked to the creek and drank some of the water then returned to extinguish his fire. He covered up the ash and residue from the fire as best as he could; he did not want to leave a trail for someone to follow. Loading his gear on his back he grabbed his rifle leaning against the tree and started to follow the blood trail leading out of the camp.

He walked slowly, stopping, taking a few steps and then moving on as his eyes scanned for anything out of the ordinary. As he trailed the bear deeper into the forest the sound of the creek diminished. He remembered Kiska warning him that a wounded bear could be very dangerous. He had traveled several more yards into the forest when he spotted a large dark object lying between three trees grown close together. Checking the wind, he was OK, crouching down he moved to within twenty feet of the animal. Squatting down he watched the flanks of the animal for any motion of breathing. Satisfied he cocked the hammer back on his rifle and slowly moved forward toward the bear. He cautiously circled the bear, and then approached from the rear. Blood seeped from a bullet hole near his left eye. Walking up to the bear, his rifle ready, he kicked the animal in the butt. The bear showed no signs of life. Looking the animal over he could see the bear was hit under the left front leg and had another hole in its rump. It was a large brown bear, probably weighing around 1,000 pounds. He was a young male and Clede more than likely had drifted into his territory. Pulling the knife Kiska gave him from the scabbard he struggled to roll the big animal on his side and began to gut the bear. He worked better than three hours to skin the hide off of the bear. Hanging the large hide in a nearby tree he cleaned the inside of the hide removing any meat. Rolling the hide up he tied leather straps from his backpack around the bearskin. He cut some of the meat from the rump of the bear; he would carry what he could for eating later. The rest he would leave for the varmints in the forest to enjoy. He attempted to lift the hide but it was too heavy so he dragged it back to the campsite.

At the creek he stooped down and washed the blood as best as he could from his clothes and cleaned his knife returning it to the sheath. He watched as the trout bit at some of the bits of meat that fell into the creek. The hide was too heavy to carry so he decided he would cut out a piece that he could use as a bedroll. Pulling his knife from its sheath he cut out the piece he desired and rolled it up and tied it to the top of his pack.

Loading his backpack and rifle in hand he once again moved north following a trail through the forest. He followed the creek upstream as it wound its way through the dense forest. The added weight of the bear hide would be worth the effort as the weather turned colder. He wanted to distance himself from the carcass and commotion he made shooting the bear. He didn't want anyone within range to know there was another soul in the area. The gunshots could be heard for many miles as the echoes bounced through the mountains. He pressed on picking up the pace as he followed the creek.

As the sun began to set Clede found a good campsite along that same creek. This time he would try and keep his campfire burning all night. He didn't desire another episode like the one he had the night before. He was fortunate indeed that he was still breathing and not a scratch on him. Setting up camp he soon had a nice fire burning. He unrolled the hide and would give it time to dry before using it. Once it dried he would beat on it with a stick to soften it up. It would come in handy in the near future. Clede hurried to put things in order; he wanted to get settled down for what he hoped would be a full night's sleep. He wanted to get an early start the next morning on his march north.

A couple of months had passed since he left Kiska and the Nootka village. The nights were much cooler and longer than when he first left. A light snow had already fallen one night, as he lay asleep. So far he had only encountered a small hunting party of Indians he saw across a canyon from his location. He hid himself behind the trees until they were well out of sight. The distance was too far and he didn't recognize the markings. Good chance this was their territory; he just wanted to pass through without detection. He sat quietly behind the tree for about an hour then when he was satisfied the coast was clear he moved on slowly. As he traveled he kept a lookout for a good place to winter. Snow was falling regularly in the higher elevations now. There was no way he would be able to construct something as elaborate as what the Nootkas built. Glancing west he saw the sun was beginning to set; he would have to set up camp pretty soon. He knew he had moved pretty far north and the winter would probably be much more severe than in the Noot village. The creek he was following dumped into a narrow river. The river wound through the saddle of two mountains for maybe three miles then it flowed into a lake. Clede changed direction and followed the lake bank around to the north. As he walked out of the forest he found what he was looking for—on the northern shore of the lake was a small valley. A large mountain loomed to the north with the dense forest coming within fifty yards of the lake. There was a beautiful lush valley between the forest and lake—this would be a good place to build his cabin. Dropping the heavy backpack to the ground he sat down on a log from a fallen tree. Reaching into his pack he took out some of his dwindling supply of jerky. There was plenty of fresh water, a forest to hunt in, and a steep mountain protecting the northern perimeter. This mountain would protect him from the northern blast of the winter storms, and anyone coming across the lake by canoe could be seen in plenty of time. Fishing from the lake should supply him with a nice fresh supply of fish. He would build his cabin just at the edge of the forest and he would try and camouflage it so that he would not be easily detected.

After finishing his jerky he untied his ax from the pack and got busy downing a few small trees he would use for a cabin. Some of the roughage he would use to construct a lean-to for tonight. By the time dark crept up on him his camp was well established and he had the base put together for his cabin. Lying under the lean-to with a fire burning near he glanced into the starry cool night. A shooting star zoomed across the sky as his mind filled with plans for the coming days. Looking at the flickering of the flames he thought about how far he had come since Alki Point. The bear hide roll felt good between himself and the hard ground. There was a reflection of the lake; he listened as a water bird from the lake sang its song in the little serene valley. Clede laid his rifle next to his side and pulled his pistol from the scabbard, laying it on his chest and placing his finger in the trigger guard. Tomorrow would be a busy day as he watched clouds move in over the mountains.

Sitting up suddenly the next morning he fought to remember what had transpired from the day before. Reaching in his backpack he pulled out the last piece of jerky. He would have to spend some time fishing or hunting today. A slight sleet was falling as the cool winds blew across the little valley then over the lake. Chewing on the jerky he strapped on his pistol and grabbed his rifle and ax. As he stood there stretching, his eyes scanned all around for any sight of something unusual. Satisfied he was completely alone he walked toward the forest. He chose young trees to make his cabin. With only his own strength he would have to use levers to roll the heavy logs into position. Finding a nice tree he set his rifle against another tree and swung his ax. The sound echoed across the lake; he would hesitate from time to time to rest and look for anyone else who might hear his chopping. Around noontime he stopped to rest and noticed the clouds of the morning were gone. Even though the air was chilly Clede had to wipe sweat from his forehead. He glanced out across the lake and saw an eagle swoop down and pick up a fish with his talons. That reminded him he needed to spend some time foraging for food before dark. Surveying his cabin he had piled the logs three high on the way to building the walls. That was enough for today, he would go fishing on the lake. Clede stopped and picked up his rifle and ax and made his way back to his campsite.

He whittled out a spear from the roughage and used his knife as the spearhead. At the lake he walked the bank edge slowly peering into the crystal clear waters for any sign of fish swimming. There he saw one hiding next to a large rock in the lake. Standing perfectly still with spear back he waited for his chance; the fish swam out from under the rock just far enough. A quick plunge with the spear and he struck the fish through the back pinning him down. He reached under the fish and brought him up wiggling to free himself. Clede backed away from the lake and let the fish slip off his spear and fall to the ground. He then untied his knife from the spear and cleaned the large fish. The fish would feed him for at least a couple of days; he wouldn't have to hunt for food soon. After cleaning the fish at the edge of the lake he washed the blood from his hands and drank some of the cold water. Back at the campsite he stoked the fire and added wood till the flames were high. He cut the fish in two large halves and placed them over the fire. He was exhausted and his bum leg ached him a bit. The leg was healed but he still would feel soreness whenever he really overextended himself. Clede knew he must hurry, he felt that the weather would change drastically soon and he wanted his cabin to be complete before the first good snow. He needed time to hunt and fish so that he would have enough food to hold him over.

A week passed and Clede's cabin slowly began to take shape. He felt proud of his accomplishment, it would keep him warm through the winter. He remembered the old mule Kiska had and wished many times he had a mule. Tomorrow he would finish the cabin with only part of the roof to complete. A snow was falling but it was light; he needed to do some fishing and hunting soon.

The next day Clede was on top of the cabin finishing the roof and patching any holes he could find when he spotted a large bull elk watering at the lake. That would give him plenty of meat for a while and with the temperatures dropping below freezing at night it would keep. Slowly grabbing his rifle he rested his arms on his legs as he squatted on the roof. Taking aim on the animal's shoulder he held his breath and slowly squeezed the trigger. A loud bang echoed through the valley as the bullet found its mark. The elk's front legs buckled as the large animal collapsed into the lake waters. Clede sat for a few minutes reloading his rifle and watching but the elk made no attempt to get up. He was dead. With his rifle in his right hand Clede jumped off the roof and walked to the elk. It was a young bull of approximately five hundred pounds, it would give him plenty of meat for a while. Pulling out his knife and standing in the edge of the lake he gutted the animal, cutting off the head and legs. Then with all the strength he could muster he managed to drag the elk onto the dry bank. He propped the animal on its back and skinned him. Clede tacked the hide to the side wall of the cabin to dry.

He would work on the hide later, he could use it. He cut the animal carcass into quarters and hung the meat in his cabin. He would eat well tonight. Working the rest of the evening he made poles to lay the meat across to dry. By nightfall he had moved inside the cabin and used a piece from his bear roll to make hinges for his door. Tomorrow he would make himself a few pieces of furniture. A fire roaring in the fireplace, he sat down on the floor on the bear hide rug. Clede looked out his door across the valley and lake but he saw no one as a light powder of snow covered the ground. Closing the door he dropped the log into place—that would lock the door from any sudden intruders. Tomorrow he would look for dead wood to chop up for the fireplace. He would need a pretty good stack of dried wood. Maybe he would work on a small storage building to keep the wood dry and store his meat like the Nootkas did. Lying in front of the fireplace watching the flames dance he slowly fell asleep.

The next day he was up early, being hungry he roasted a piece of elk meat over the fire in the fireplace. Then as the sun rose in the east he grabbed his rifle and ax and made his way to the forest. He worked all day building the storage room next to his cabin where he would store wood and food. Just as he had learned from the Nootkas he cut a small hole just big enough so that he could move between the two buildings. Then the following day he spent cutting up wood to store in his new makeshift building. While back in the forest he came upon a black bear, which he promptly downed with his Hawkens. He cleaned and skinned the bear, putting the meat in the storage room and tacking the hide outside to dry. Finishing up as the sun set in the west Clede felt good at all he had accomplished. He piled the last of the logs along the outside wall of the cabin. He could always bring that wood in to replenish what he had stored in the storage building. As he did every evening he stood outside the doorway and searched his little valley and across the lake for any signs of another human being. Sleet was falling mixed with light snow when he returned to his cabin after a full day. He would make some furniture for his cabin but that would be for another day. He would use the bear oil from the black bear to cover his boots. The wet cold snow seeping into his boots could cause frostbite. Satisfied he was secure in his little valley he closed the door on another day.

The next morning as he was chewing on a piece of meat that was left over, he sat by the fireplace whittling on a branch that he had cut the day before. Clede fashioned a spear point with a barb from the leg bone of the elk. Then he tied the spear point to the shaft with leather strips. The spear completed he grabbed his rifle and swung open the cabin door. Three inches of snow covered the valley from the night before. Knowing it was not cold enough for the lake to freeze over he decided he would spend his day fishing. Shutting the door he walked down to the edge of the lake and spotted a cluster of reeds growing along the bank. Squatting over so not to cast his shadow on the water, he laid his bag and rifle down beside him. With his spear in his right hand he slowly walked into the edge of the waters looking for any movement of a fish. He spotted a large brown trout swimming along the edge of the reeds. Cocking the spear back he stood motionless and waited for the fish to move into position. Throwing the spear suddenly he saw blood spread in the water and felt the fish wiggling as he had him pinned to the bottom. Slowly lifting the big trout the barb was doing its job as he lifted the spear up and looked at the fish. Pulling the fish free he tossed him far upon the bank. He continued till he had three trout flopping on the bank then he decided that was enough for now. He would clean and scale these and put them in his bag before returning to fish for more.

As he sat cleaning the fish he glanced up and saw something on the distant horizon. Dropping to the ground he crawled on his belly to his rifle then lifted his head to look over the terrain. As he continued to watch the horizon letting his eyes clear he saw an Indian on horseback just in the edge of the forest. An Indian with a single eagle feather tied to his braided hair. The Indian sat motionless on his horse staring at Clede's cabin. The light curl of smoke coming from the fireplace must have attracted his attention. A cold chill ran down Clede's back with the thought that someone else knew he was in the valley. Putting a bead on the Indian he slowly cocked the hammer back as he contemplated whether he should shoot him or not. What if there were others, or if he shot this one would others come looking for him? His heart pounded with anxiety as he tried to make up his mind, which would be the best course of action. Straining his eyes he did not recognize the markings on the Indian or his horse. The Indian just sat rigid on the horse watching the cabin. Sweat broke out on Clede's forehead as he held the bead on the Indian's chest. Then the Indian turned his horse and looked out across the lake but Clede was too well hidden for him to see him. The Indian then turned his horse and disappeared into the forest.

Clede cussed to himself; had he made the right decision? He could only hope now that the Indian would move on and not bring trouble for him. The secure feeling he had enjoyed since entering the valley had now been shattered. From now on he would have to be alert. There was not enough time for him to move and rebuild, it was too late in the fall for that now. Clede lay there for well over an hour before he finally sat up and started gathering the fish and his stuff together. He didn't want to kill the Indian but maybe he should have. Then he stood up and scanned 360 degrees around him and only when he was sure no one was there he moved toward his cabin. At the door he stopped and looked again, no way for him to know if the Indian was back in the forest watching him. Well, as long as it was a single Indian he figured he could take care of himself. His worry was if the Indian brought a bunch of his buddies. Closing the door he locked it behind himself.

He didn't have enough time to catch as much fish as he would have liked. There was enough fish to eat on for at least a few days before he would try and fish again—this was proving to be a bad day. Filleting the fish he stuck some of it over the fire, the rest he hung from the roof in his storage room. A nice roaring fire would keep him snug from the cold outside. Clede couldn't sleep, his thoughts kept returning to the rider that rode into his valley. So he sat by the fire eating some of the tasty trout and working on a chair. Blowing on the fish to cool it before putting it into his mouth. Occasionally stopping to pull out a bone, which he tossed into the fire. Most of the elk and some of the bear he made into jerky that hung in his storage. Finishing his chair he sat down in it to try it out. It seemed sturdy enough and it was good to be off the dirt floor. He whittled out a drinking cup, throwing the shavings into the fire. Then he poured water into his wooden cup. He made the elk's stomach into a water bag. Tomorrow he would work on a table, he thought as he prepared for bed. He listened for several minutes but the only noise he heard was the blowing of the wind outside. Sounded like another storm and by the sound of it this one was bigger than the last. Lying on his blanket next to the fire he pulled the bear hide up over his waist. With his rifle at his side and his pistol on his chest he closed his eyes, visualizing the Indian he saw earlier today. He could only hope that it didn't mean trouble for him.

Awakened by the noticeable chill in the cabin he stumbled in the darkness to the pile of logs. Adding wood to the fireplace and stirring up the live coals he soon had a roaring fire. Sitting in his chair he could hear the wind still blowing strong outside. Soon the cabin began to warm and he decided to peek outside. With his hand on his pistol he approached the door. Lifting the lock he pushed but found the door was stuck. He tried again, this time with more effort, and the door moved some. Then he shoved on it hard and the door pried open just enough for him to look out. About a foot of snow had fallen during the night and some of it stung his face as it blew through the door. Dropping down on all fours he scraped the snow away from the door enough to open it wider. He could scarcely see the lake for the blowing snow; quickly he pulled the door shut and locked it. This would be a good day to stay inside, he could work on a cot and a table today. Another thought crossed his mind—he remembered Kiska telling him sometimes they would cut a door in the roof to be able to get out if the snow became too deep. After breakfast Clede spent the day constructing a table and a cot. He would use the brown bear hide for a mattress on his cot and the black bear hide he would use to cover himself. They would keep him warm on very cold nights. The winds blew all day and the snows fell into the valley. The cabin kept him warm from the harsh elements outside. His mind returned to the Indian of the day before. He was pretty sure if the Indian had friends they wouldn't bother him on a day such as this. Clede had no desire to fight, he just wanted to winter here then he would be on his way again.

The next morning the winds calmed and Clede decided to cut a hole in the roof. He went out through the front door and climbed on the roof to construct an escape door should the snow become too deep to use the main door. This gave him a means to escape. He made a frame on the inside so that the door could be opened and then shut. He worked all day, stopping only to warm himself occasionally. While up on the roof he would stop and scan the valley, lake and forest for any signs of the Indian. No sight of him—maybe he was just passing through, he could only hope. Clede made a small ladder so that he could push the door open from inside. He also made a means by which he could lock this door from inside. After finishing the job he opened and closed the door several times to check it. It worked perfectly. With his rifle and ax in hand Clede jumped down from the roof into the deep snow. He then scraped the snow away from the main door with the butt of his rifle. There were snowdrifts piled against the side of the wall from the high winds that blew that night before. Returning through the main door he shut and secured it. He crawled up the ladder and secured the roof hatch, then he warmed his hands over the open flames of the fireplace.

With a few hours of daylight left till dark he decided to make a swing along the forest edge to check for tracks or any sign of the Indian. It worried him that he had been detected. He checked his boots to see if they were dry; he had rubbed some of the bear grease on them earlier. Feeling for his pistol on his side it was tied taut to his leg. Grabbing his coat from his cot he put it on and then slipped the powder horn strap over his head. Picking up his rifle and unlocking the main door he stepped outside and closed the door behind him. Standing still he slowly scanned the tree line all the way to the lake. A light snow still fell from the heavily overcast skies as he turned right and walked just inside the tree line. Clede knew the chances of finding any signs would be almost nil because of the snowfall. But still he needed to reassure himself, plus getting out of the cabin for a while would be good for his spirits. He could also check the traps he set near the creek that flowed into the lake. Clede didn't know much about trapping but he'd bought several traps anyway. He figured he could learn and the money from the furs would help him replenish his powder, shot and caps. One thing for sure, he wouldn't go to Alki Point, he was a long way from there anyway.

The snow crunched under his boots as he very slowly walked, squatting down occasionally to scan back into the forest then across the valley toward the lake. He moved on in this fashion until he reached the west shore of the lake. No signs of a human at all, only a few deer prints were visible. The wet snow seeped into his boots even though he had greased them down well. Looking into the sky there was only maybe another hour before dark. He turned around and headed back across the valley toward his cabin in the distance. A small curl of smoke lifted then was caught by the wind and disappeared. Reaching his first trap he pulled it from the partially frozen lake. Nothing in the trap—the bait was gone and nothing. Trapping seemed to be more difficult than he thought it would be. Squatting down he reset the trap and slowly eased it back into the frigid waters. Then he stood up, looked all around and moved on to the next trap. Same result in each trap, but he wouldn't get discouraged, he knew that he would eventually learn the art of trapping.

As time passed he was once again becoming more secure in his cabin that was hidden in the little valley by the emerald lake. He returned to the cabin, it was still twilight by the time he reached the door. Hesitating he took one long look, opened the door and secured it. In the cabin he stoked the fire and added wood then he hung his coat and powder horn on a wooden peg on the wall. He laid his rifle on his table and sat down, taking his boots and socks off and placing them near the fire to dry. Next he pulled some of the meat that was left over from the last meal and chewed on the dry meat. He sat there watching the fire flicker and listening to the wind blowing again outside. It was good to get out for a while. Clede had overheard from some in Alki Point about trappers and gold hunters going mad cooped up in their cabins. He pulled his knife out and sharpened it on a stone, then returned it to its sheath. Clede felt chilled and thought about the bottle of scotch he bought back in Alki Point. That would sure taste good with the meat and help to warm him. Opening his bag he bulled the bottle out and cut the top from the bottle. He poured some of the liquid into his cup and drank it slowly. The warmth of it could be felt as it proceeded to his stomach. He sealed the bottle and put it on the table; he would only take a drink to warm himself. Next he unbuckled his pistol and put it next to the scotch on the table. Clede felt the effects of the scotch—he was not used to drinking, he felt mellow and warm. A piece of ice fell from the trap door to the dirt floor. He knew it must have been snowing again outside. His mind took him back to the winter he spent with the Nootkas. Clede wondered how they were doing and if they were still living in the same place. Pulling the pistol out he lay back on the cot laying the pistol on his chest. He watched the shadows jumping over the roof from the flickering fire then he closed his eyes and went to sleep.

The storm had really intensified during the long night. Awakening slowly and wiping the back of his hand across his eyes he attempted to clear his vision. Sitting up on the side of his bunk he shoved the pistol back into its scabbard on the table. He knew it was still early—it wouldn't be daylight for another couple of hours. Clede got up and put some more wood on the fire then he crawled through the hole into the storage room. He brought more wood out to add to the pile near the fireplace. He would have to hunt again soon, his food supply was dwindling. Picking up a piece of wood he pulled out his knife and began to whittle on it. Several hours passed as he intently worked on the piece of wood and it began to take shape in the form of an eagle. A pile of shavings lay at his feet as he made the final few adjustments to it. Then with the point of his knife he drilled a small hole in the back of the eagle. Taking a leather string from his backpack he cut it long enough to hang the eagle around his neck. Clede tied the ends and slipped it over his head and let it drop onto his chest. He loved to watch eagles as they soared so gracefully in the skies, sometimes swooping down to grab a fish in their talons. He wondered how it would be to be able to soar over the mountains; he wondered if man might one day fly.

Standing up and brushing the shavings from his buckskin pants he buckled his pistol to his side. Checking his socks and boots to see if they were dry he sat down and put them on. Next he took his hat from a peg and screwed it down on his head then tried the main door but it was stuck. He tried shoving it with all his might but it wouldn't budge. Then he crawled up the ladder, unlocked the trap door and shoved on it. It gave a little so he shoved hard and it swung open dumping snow on his hat. The wind blew the snow in his face, stinging it like a swarm of bees. He quickly turned his face away from the direction of the wind. Using his hand he brushed the snow back from the trap door then stepped out onto the roof in the dim light of morning. He could barely see the lake but he knew it was nearly frozen over except for a hole in the center. Carefully he walked over and looked down at his main door. He could see why he couldn't get out—the snow was maybe three or four foot deep there. No use to clear the snow from it until it stopped. Returning to the trap door he cleared the snow back as best as he could from around the door. He glanced across the forest and valley and thought no human in his right mind would be out in this. A real blizzard was kicking up for sure—he hoped it wouldn't last too much longer. Stepping onto the ladder he pulled the door shut behind him and then secured it. The floor was muddy at the base of the ladder from the melted snow. With his right boot he scraped dirt from other parts of the room into a pile. Then he scooped the dirt up in his hand and covered the wetness on the floor. No doubt in his mind, he was socked in until this storm eased.

Clede kept as busy as he could to pass away the hours of boredom. He cleaned his pistol and rifle then sewed up some bad places in his bear coat. Next he checked the storage room and saw that the meat was nearly frozen solid. He brought a large chunk of jerky into the cabin and hung it up so it would be edible and not frozen. After this he scraped some of the snow from the roof and added it to his water bag so that he would have plenty of fresh water. He still had a pretty good supply of wood but he could go out later and bring some in from his stock along the cabin wall outside if needed. His next task was whittling out a spoon, then he made a few more pegs to hang his hat and pistol on and then sat down for his evening meal.

Chapter 4

The storm continued to rage for three days with no letup in sight. Clede tried to maintain some of his sanity but could feel cabin fever making him jittery. Then the start of the fourth day the winds slowed. He heard a rapping sound coming from the corner of the roof that caught his curiosity. Maybe an animal was trying to dig through the roof to find some warmth below? He needed more firewood and getting out of the cabin for a while would help his jitters. He pushed hard against the main door with his shoulder but it wouldn't move. The trap door looked like his only option. Slipping into his coat, buckling his pistol tight around his waist he bent over and tied the leather strings to his leg. Then he took his hat from a peg and screwed it down and grabbed his rifle. Leaning it against the ladder he took two steps up the ladder and unlocked the trap door. It felt really heavy but with determined strength he slowly began to push it open. A large pile of snow fell into the cabin as he pushed the door back. Bending over he reached for his rifle then he took another step and peered over the roof. He could see nothing but snow piled up in every direction. This had really been a bad storm; it was good to have a break. Taking one more step he then stepped onto the roof with his right boot. There was about two feet of snow covering the roof. He took a 360-degree scan but he could see nothing moving.

Remembering the rapping on the roof he looked toward the corner of the roof where he had heard the noise. An unusually large pile of snow lay there. Pulling the hammer back on his rifle he slowly approached the pile of snow. As he neared the figure he could see that it wasn't an animal but a human being almost completely submerged in the snow. With his right boot he kicked the feet of the individual but he showed no signs of life. Squatting down Clede brushed the snow away from his head—he could see it was an Indian from his clothes. Checking his breathing he could see it was very shallow. Letting the hammer down on his Hawkens he lay it down on the roof. Reaching under the Indian's arms he drug the Indian to the trap door, dropping him there. Then he went back and picked up his rifle and took it down inside and set it against the wall. Back up on the roof he picked the Indian up and worked his feet down the ladder first. Holding him up by the arms he stepped down the ladder and let the man go at the bottom. Clede reached back and shut the trap door locking it behind him.

On the floor he picked the Indian up and drug him over close to the fireplace. He added wood to the fire and as it came to a roar a cold shiver went down his spine. This was the same Indian he had seen on horseback that was checking out his cabin. Grabbing his bear hide from his cot he threw it over the Indian. Clede reached up and cut a piece of jerky and then sat down in his chair. Chewing on the meat he pondered what he should do. For sure he better not let his guard down—there was no way for him to know what reaction would come from the man when and if he came to. The Indian groaned and Clede put his hand on his pistol in anticipation but he didn't move. As he sat there studying the Indian he saw his problem. His left leg was broken. Clede decided he would set his leg. He took a log from the woodpile and using his ax, he split it. Taking the two splints he tied them tightly to his leg—this was all he knew to do for him. Clede filled his cup with water then sat back down at the table to finish up his jerky.

The time passed slowly as Clede sat watching the Indian. About ten hours had passed since he brought the Indian into his cabin. He felt tired and sleepy but he was afraid to doze off. To keep from falling asleep he would add wood to the fire, check on the Indian, anything to keep himself awake. Clede bent down and checked his forehead—he was warm and his breathing was normal and steady. Returning to his chair he sat back and tried to relax. Several more hours passed and Clede dozed off sitting in the chair. Suddenly he was awakened by a noise in the cabin. He grabbed for his pistol and he saw the Indian sitting up. They stared at each other for a few seconds then the Indian shakily fell back into unconsciousness again. Clede let the hammer down on his pistol and laid it on the table. Another hour passed then he noticed the Indian lying there looking around. Clede stood up and the Indian's eyes watched his every move. Putting his fingers to his mouth Clede asked him if he were hungry. The Indian nodded his head slightly. Clede pulled his knife from the sheath on his left side and cut off a piece of the jerky. He cautiously handed the piece of meat to the Indian. The Indian sat up and chewed on the jerky watching Clede's every move. Pouring more water into his cup he offered it to the Indian. The man drank the water in gulps, drinking two cups full before handing it back to Clede.

Clede sat motionless watching him eat, saying nothing. The Indian slowly worked his way to his feet but groaned and hopped on his right leg when he realized he had a broken leg. Clede pointed at his cot, and the Indian hopped over and sat down on it. The Indian pointed at his leg and Clede understood this is what brought him to his cabin. With crude hand signs they were able to understand each other to some extent. Clede understood enough to know that the Indian had fallen from his horse, breaking his leg. Remembering the cabin the Indian hoped to find shelter there but by the time he pulled himself up on the roof he was nearly frozen. Then Clede spoke, he pointed at himself and said, "Clede."

The Indian pointed at himself and said, "Keewatin."

Both men began to relax around each other, as they both realized neither intended harm to the other. They communicated in this fashion for several hours. The best Clede could tell the Indian was not a local native. His tribe was the Yellowknifes, their territory was many moons north of their location. Keewatin became shaky and Clede motioned for him to lay back and sleep. The Indian nodded and lay back on Clede's cot, falling a sleep quickly. Clede felt much more secure now that he had talked to Keewatin and learned something about him. He speculated that Keewatin's horse must have thrown him in the storm, breaking his leg. No telling what happened to his horse in this blizzard. The tips of his ears and fingers were slightly frostbitten but he was young and strong, he would recover with some rest and food.

Keewatin told Clede he was in search of a great white bear. This bear had magical powers that the Indian could have if he could kill this bear. Clede knew the Indians could have many mythical spirits and animals in their culture. In any case it was good to have another human being's company, even if neither could speak the other's language. Clede lay down on the floor next to the fireplace and dozed off; he felt secure that the Indian meant him no harm. Perhaps Keewatin would prove to be just as good a friend as Kiska had been.

Two weeks had passed since Clede brought Keewatin into his cabin to nurse him back to good health. With the addition of the Indian his meat supply was running dangerously low. Clede dressed in his coat, hat, powder horn, backpack, and pistol, plus rifle in his right hand and spear in his left, and he climbed the ladder to the roof. Keewatin was sitting in his chair staring into the fire. He looked up and nodded as Clede shut the trap door. The sun was shining bright across the snow-covered roof and the sky was crystal clear. It had been many days since Clede had seen the sun. As he sucked in a deep breath of the fresh air it burned his lungs. A large puff of smoke blew from his mouth as he breathed back out again. Screwing his hat down tight he grabbed his rifle in his right hand and jumped from the roof. He walked around to the main door and brushed the snow away with the butt of his rifle. He could see that the lake was frozen over; he would try and cut through it using his ax. Clede sat down and put on the snowshoes he made back during the storm; he thought they would come in handy. Using his rifle to support himself he stood up and took a few steps. He would go slowly until he got the feel of snowshoes on his boots.

Once he reached the lake he stopped and made a careful check in all directions—he was alone. His traps were frozen under the ice, he would retrieve them in the spring when the ice melted. Cautiously he checked the ice. It seemed plenty thick enough to hold his weight. He walked about twenty yards out on the ice pack and then dropped his backpack on the ice. Laying his rifle next to the pack he bent over and untied his ax. Chopping at the ice he cut a hole about twelve inches in diameter into it. He could see that the ice on the lake was about eight inches thick, plenty strong enough to hold him. Clede put a piece of meat on a leather strand and dropped it into the water to lure a fish. Squatting on his knees he held the leather strand in his left hand and the spear drawn back in the ready position in his right. After several minutes passed he saw the shadowy figure of a large lake trout as he circled the piece of meat. Taking aim he thrust the spear into the hole, jabbing the fish in the side. Quickly he jerked the spear back with the fish wiggling to free himself from the barb. Turning to the side he worked the fish from his spear letting him flop violently on the ice. He then dropped the meat back into the hole and reset himself for another. He fished for about two hours and managed to catch six large trout. Laying the spear down he pulled his knife from his side and scaled and gutted the fish. Dropping the guts into the hole he could see a lot of action as other fish came for the feast. Clede bent over and washed his hands and knife wiping them on his buckskin shirt. Then he picked up his stuff and holding the spear and rifle in his left hand he swung the trout over his right shoulder. Tied together he allowed them to hang from his shoulder. He slowly walked back to the cabin.

Clede tried the front door and it swung open. Turning around he made a good look across the valley, then he saw them. There were a set of footprints in the snow. He hurriedly entered the cabin. As his eyes adjusted to the darkness he looked around and Keewatin was gone. Dropping the fish onto the table he surveyed the room—his black bear hide, bow and arrows were missing. He leaned his spear against the wall and hung his pack on a peg. Clede pulled his pistol from his side and cocked the hammer as he closed and secured the door. On hands and knees he checked the storage room but Keewatin was gone. Those were his tracks that led from the main door toward the forest. Damn, that was some hospitality—Keewatin didn't even say thanks. Most of the jerky he had left was also gone.

He picked up the fish, all but one, and hung them on the poles to dry. Then he added wood to the fireplace and placed the fish over the fire to cook. Keewatin's tracks had headed toward the forest then straight north up over the mountains behind the cabin. Clede murmured to himself, "I hope you can climb that mountain with that broken leg." He was angry with himself for trusting the damn Indian. *Oh well, nothing to do now he's gone. Glad I could help him, he was a goner for sure,* he thought.

Clede took off his coat and hat and hung them up, then his attention turned to the fish roasting on the fire. He poured some water into his cup and pulled the table and chair near the warmth of the fire. Then he sat down and warmed his hands over the fire. Checking the fish he found it was nearly done. His taste buds watered, it had been awhile since he had any fresh meat. *Wonder what month this is,* he thought, *maybe March, don't think it is April yet.* It had sure been a tough winter, it would have been impossible to make it without this cabin. He hoped the weather would hold so he could go hunting tomorrow. *The fish won't last me long, even without Keewatin to feed.* He reached down and pulled some of the meat from the filet and slowly chewed it then swallowed it. The fish tasted real good for a change. Maybe it was a custom of the Yellowknifes never to say good-bye; the Indians had some funny ways all right.

Right before dark he brought in the remainder of the wood along the wall. He spotted a buck along the tree line just west of the lake while fetching the wood. *I'll hunt over in that area where I saw the buck,* he thought. *It's going to be real cold tonight with those clear skies.* Back in the cabin he finished off the fish and drank a sip of the scotch. Once again he felt secure in this valley. He was pretty sure Keewatin had meant him no harm. He wiped his pistol, rifle and sharpened his knife before turning in. He'd have to use his Indian blanket since he didn't have his black bear hide any longer. Clede sat down on his cot and pulled his boots off and pulled the pistol from its scabbard and put it on his chest as he called it a day.

Rising early the next day before it was daylight Clede strapped on his gun belt and knife and put on his weather-worn boots. He stooped down and crawled into his storage room; there was just one small bit of jerky left. Crawling back out he wrapped the meat in his bandana and packed it in his backpack. When he had finished packing his backpack he put his coat and hat on and grabbed his Hawkens on the way to the main door. Unlocking the door and swinging it gently open he could see that it was just breaking day. He stepped out and shut the door behind him as he waited for his eyes to adjust to the darkness. The stars were still visible and a quarter moon hung low across the frozen lake. He shivered from the cold as he buttoned his coat up around his neck. A wolf hollered in the mountains behind his cabin. He made one more check to make sure he had everything; he was ready.

It felt good to venture out and do some hunting, being cooped up in the cabin could make you edgy. Clede slipped into his snowshoes then as the sky lightened in anticipation of the sunrise he moved toward the forest. There were clouds forming just over the mountains to the north, it looked like another storm was coming. It was still some distance away, probably wouldn't reach him till sometime around dark. Stopping and looking toward his cabin he saw it was all but invisible buried in the deep snow, just a small stream of smoke could be seen. He would follow the lake bank looking for tracks from the buck he seen the day before. Once he located them he would follow them into the forest.

It took him better than an hour to reach the western side of the lake because of the deep snow. He spotted the tracks and very slowly began to follow them back into the forest. Walking Indian style he would crouch down and look for legs or any dark form against the white background. Several hundred yards back into the forest he spotted a heavily traveled trail that the deer were following. Finding a strategic position against a tree he took his backpack off and dropped it next to the tree. Brushing back the snow from the base of the tree with his boot he sat down and cradled his rifle across his lap. From this position there were several trails that came together; with a little luck maybe he could catch a deer on the move. The wind blew in his face so they would not be able to catch his scent. Using the tree as a background he would blend into the trunk of the tree. Leaning his head back against the tree he sat motionless waiting for the chance to make a shot. Clede had rubbed some of the cold ashes from the fireplace to darken his white face. He slowly turned his head and eyes looking for motion of any kind in the forest.

The sky was clouding up now and a small breeze began to blow; a few flurries fell and gently found their way to the forest floor. He could see a creek flowing from the side of the mountain that came through the forest and down to the lake. A small patch of frozen grass near the creek was what the deer were looking for. There wasn't much for them to eat during these times but they had pawed out a few morsels of last year's greenery. As he studied the trail and grass he caught movement from his right eye back in the forest. Turning his head very slowly he could see it was a large buck following the trail with his head down. Clede started to slowly bring the Hawkens to his shoulder but froze when the buck raised his head and then cocked his ears for any sound. Several seconds passed then the animal dropped his head and continued to paw in the snow for something to eat. He continued on and soon had the butt of the rifle in his shoulder and his cheek resting on the cold iron of the barrel. The buck turned sideways to Clede to paw in the snow off the trail. He took careful aim, held his breath then slowly exhaled and squeezed the trigger. The Hawkens jumped into his shoulder and banged loudly sending smoke toward the buck into the forest. The buck doubled up and bolted, fell to his knees then laboriously regained its balance and trotted into the cover of the forest.

Grumbling to himself Clede was sure his aim was true but it was hard for him to hold steady shivering in the cold. Normally they drop in their tracks when the fifty-caliber ball hits them. Relaxing he reloaded his rifle as he listened for sounds of the wounded animal. He could only hear the ringing in his ear from the discharge of the rifle. The best thing for him would be to sit tight for maybe half an hour or so to let the deer lie down and bleed out. The buck was hit well, he could tell by the way he fell to his knees and struggled to regain his stance. Clede reached down and cupped some of the snow in his hand and ate it. When he figured he had sat long enough he pushed himself up using his rifle. Standing there for a moment to allow the blood to return to his legs he bent down and picked up his backpack. With his rifle in his right hand he walked to where he had shot the deer.

Nearing the site he noticed a limb cut into and hanging down. Now he knew why the buck hadn't fallen in his tracks, the bullet had been diverted some when it hit the limb. He hadn't noticed that limb when he squeezed the trigger. At the place where the buck fell there was hair, lots of blood and bone fragments. The blood was a bright pink—that told him his bullet got into the animal's lungs. The tree limb caused him to miss the heart, bending the bullet in a lower trajectory. Lots of blood left an easy trail to follow; he figured the animal couldn't have gone too far. He followed the animal walking very slowly he didn't want to spook the animal up from where he probably was lying. The buck hadn't tried to climb the mountain but in its weakened condition had drifted downward instead.

As Clede crept along slowly approximately two hundred yards from where he shot the buck he spotted the deer. When he was fifteen feet from the buck the deer suddenly got up and lunged forward with head down. Clede had no time to react, the deer ran straight into him knocking his rifle from his hand. He felt a terrible pain in his right leg as the deer thrust a horn into him knocking him backward. Quickly he grabbed the horns with his right hand and jerked his knife out with his left. With a sweeping motion he came up under the throat of the deer and jerked the knife back, cutting the buck's throat. The deer fell partially on Clede. He groaned as the horn pulled at his leg as the buck jerked. Blood from the deer and Clede's leg covered the snow.

Lying still for a moment he fought to regain his composure as the pain slowly subsided some. Sitting up in the snow he grabbed the antlers of the dead buck and worked the horn from his leg. His pants were soaked from the blood that ran from the wound. Slipping his arms out of his backpack he pulled his bandana out. Using it as a tourniquet he tied it tight cutting off some of the blood flow. Pushing the buck off of him he struggled to his feet. He bent over with a lot of pain and picked up a small stick and put it through the bandana, twisting it to tighten it even more. Standing there for a few moments he couldn't believe he had been so stupid as to approach the animal from the front. He was in trouble and he knew it; he had to get back to the cabin and treat the wound. The meat was important also; he would cut a ham from the animal and drag it behind him. Once his leg was tended to he would come back for the rest. Clede cut the ham from the buck, then tied one end of a leather strap to the hoof and the other around his waist. He put his knife back in the sheath then looking around he picked up his rifle and headed for the cabin that was about a mile away through the deep snow.

Loaded down and with much difficulty he made his way toward the cabin in the distance. The going was very slow and periodically he would stop to release the tourniquet. It began to snow heavily as he struggled leaving a trail of blood in the snow behind him. Falling once he got up and cut a limb from a tree and made a crutch to help him maintain his balance. After traveling for an hour he was still five or six hundred yards from the cabin. He was so weak he couldn't carry the ham any longer so he cut the strap that held the meat. As he moved on his head became light and in his dizzy condition he fell and lay in the snow for a few moments. Grabbing a handful of the snow he rubbed it in his face then it took all his might just to get back on his feet. Stumbling in a blind fury he moved on then he saw it, the cabin door just a few feet more. It was almost dark by the time he reached the front door, and he fell into the door knocking it open as he collapsed on the floor. Using his left foot he pushed the door closed. Unhooking the backpack he let it loose on the floor behind him. Crawling to the fireplace he picked up and threw several logs into the fire then passed out.

No way for him to know how long he lay on the floor but he eventually came to. He knew he had lost quite a bit of blood; he had to stop the bleeding if he were going to survive. Pulling his knife from its sheath he cut his pants to expose the wound. It was nasty all right. Leaning over he laid the knife blade in the flames. Several minutes passed and the blade became glowing red then he took the stick that was in the tourniquet and put it between his teeth. Picking up the knife blade he took a big breath and pushed the side of the blade against the wound. The smell of burning flesh filled the air in the cabin as Clede shook in pain then passed out.

When he came to he reached up on the table and grabbed the bottle of scotch. He poured some of it on the wound and then took a very big drink. His head spun from the loss of blood and the scotch. He set the bottle against the table leg and reached for the Indian blanket pulling it over him. Head spinning he fell back into an unconscious state of mind. As he lay in the room he lost track of time as a fever wracked his body then he drifted in and out of delirium. He was on the battlefield again and men were crying and dying, then his mind went to the Nootka village, then his home and his parents.

Suddenly he opened his eyes and wondered for a moment if maybe he was dead. Slowly his blurred vision began to clear and he felt the pain in his leg and remembered what had happened. He noticed he was in his cot and wondered how he could have gotten there in his delirious state. He remembered the deer, and cauterizing the wound—as he looked around, the cabin was spinning, he wondered how long had he been out? As he lay still his eyes caught sight of the fireplace roaring away—that puzzled him. Then he saw a shadowy figure coming toward him, he was not alone. He struggled to rise up off the cot but he felt a hand on his shoulder pushing him back down. He was startled for a second but then he recognized who was sharing the cabin with him—it was Keewatin.

Keewatin motioned in sign language for him to lie still, that all was all right. The Indian must have put him in his cot, but why did he return? Then from the corner of his eye near the fireplace was someone else moving. A female, she was cooking something in the fireplace. He could tell she was very young. Keewatin said, "Tahou." The young woman approached Clede on the cot and squatted down on her knees next to where he lay. In her hands was a bowl of some substance. Uncovering his wound she rubbed the stuff into it; it burned and he grimaced in pain. She then covered the wound and got up and returned to the food cooking on the fire. Keewatin sat in his chair next to Clede and began to tell him what had transpired. He said that he and the young girl came looking for him and found him delirious on the floor. His wound was very bad and his fever very high Clede was near death. Keewatin found the deer ham lying outside of the cabin, he followed Clede's trail and found the rest of the buck in the forest. Tahou returned to Clede and fed him some of the soup that she was cooking. As he drank the liquid in the bowl he noticed the young Indian girl was a very beautiful young woman. He wondered if this was Keewatin's woman. Clede felt very weak from the fever and loss of blood—it would take him awhile to recover. Keewatin said something to Tahou and she returned to her tasks. The two men continued to talk. Clede asked if the woman was Keewatin's. Keewatin told him she was a slave girl that belonged to him she was from the Chipewyan tribe. He captured her in a raid as a child and she belonged to him and was his slave. Clede had heard rumors that some of the tribes in these parts made slaves of their captures. She couldn't be more the fourteen or fifteen years old but that was the age most Indian girls became brides. The women could be treated like cattle or horses and were traded between families. Clede felt very tired and Keewatin could sense this and motioned for him to rest. This Indian and his slave girl had saved his life; he was glad to have him as a friend.

Two days had passed and with the good care of the young slave girl Clede began to regain his strength. He could now sit up for short periods and even feed himself. The wound to his leg was healing nicely and Keewatin and he would sit and talk. Clede explained to Keewatin that being short on food and seeing the buck near the lake he had decided to go out to hunt. He told him how his bullet had hit a limb, changing the trajectory. He continued to tell him how he had come upon the dying buck and that he had lunged into him without warning. Keewatin told him he knew something was wrong when he returned to find his main door unlocked. He said Clede was very delirious when they found him and with the help of Tahou they had placed him on his cot. The Indian was pleased that he could repay Clede for saving his life also. Yes, Clede was very lucky that the two came along when they did. Perhaps another few hours and he would've been pushing up daisies.

Keewatin began to explain about Tahou. He said she was from the Chipewyan tribe. They had attacked this tribe of Chipewyans in retaliation for an earlier attack on their village. Keewatin had grabbed the very young girl and rode off with her because they stole horses from him. Clede watched his hands as the Indian told his story in sign language. The way these Indians lived was different yet in many ways not so different from the white man's. Clede was not ready for what the Indian was about to tell him. Keewatin told him the young girl called Tahou was a gift from him. He said that she was his. Clede sat motionless for a moment then he thanked Keewatin for such a great gift. Little did Keewatin know that Clede had very little need or want for a woman. When Keewatin left that day he knew he must repay Clede for saving his life. His friend needed a companion, someone to follow him on his journey through life. Little did Keewatin know that he would find his friend near death on the floor of the cabin. Clede's mind raced—he must come up with a gift for Keewatin also. He remembered his father's handmade pipe from the old country. Clede had learned from the Nootkas that the Indians considered a pipe a sacred part of their worship. Standing up and using his spear for support he hobbled over to his backpack. Opening the flap and digging down in the left corner he brought out the pipe wrapped in a cloth. Returning to his cot he sat down and unwrapped the beautifully hand-carved pipe. Clede handed it to Keewatin and signaled that this was his gift to him. The Indian grinned and he knew that his gift was an equal in his eyes.

Keewatin would leave the next day. His only reason for the journey back was to bring the girl for his good friend. Tahou packed Keewatin's Na Hcleth. This was a bag that could have religious artifacts, food, and any item that was considered important to the individual. Na Hcleth was the Chipewyan word for a bag that was usually made from the stomach of an animal. Keewatin had gone hunting at daybreak and returned with several snowshoe rabbits and a deer. This should hold his friend and Tahou until Clede was strong enough to hunt for himself.

Later in the day the two men gathered at the fireplace. Keewatin and Tahou helped Clede sit down on the floor on the Indian blanket. Keewatin retrieved the pipe that Clede gave him as a gift. The tobacco they would use was from Clede's father's private stock, which Clede gave him also. Keewatin packed the tobacco in the cup of the pipe and lit it from a stick. He took a puff and then brushed the smoke back across the top of his head. Then he passed the pipe to Clede, who followed the Indian's example. The smoke hung like a cloud in the room as the men took turns puffing on the pipe. Tahou sat in the chair at the table and watched the ritual. Keewatin sang a song in his language and raised the pipe above his head. Then he beckoned Tahou to sit next to Clede, tying their wrists together and chanting a few words—this meant that she belonged to his friend. The ceremony lasted about an hour then Keewatin dumped the pipe into the fireplace and put it in his Na Hcleth bag. It was late and Clede was tired from a long day. Keewatin and Tahou helped him back onto his feet and he hobbled to the cot, collapsing in exhaustion. He slipped into a restful sleep as he listened to the two talking softly.

Clede was awakened the next morning when Tahou shook his shoulder. The young girl, who was mature far beyond her age, handed him a bowl of meat mixed with other things he'd rather not ask about. He looked around and Keewatin was nowhere in sight. Motioning to Tahou he asked her in sign language where was his friend. She told him that he was gone. Just as before, Keewatin left without a word, just disappeared without saying good-bye. Tahou told him this was the way of the Yellowknifes, which did not believe in good-byes. That would be the last time he would ever see his friend again.

Clede watched Tahou as she went about her chores; she stirred something in him that scared him to death. He could trade her for supplies, maybe a mule, when he visited a trading post in the future. Tahou paid very little attention to him as she busily took care of the things that needed to be done. She stopped at mealtimes to eat and offer food to Clede. She would check the wound periodically, cleaning it and adding some of the medicine that she prepared earlier. He knew it was healing fast because the stuff that Tahou put on it no longer burned. A thought crossed his mind that since she was a slave girl she might stick a knife in him while he slept or just sneak out and run back to her people. All of this wasn't his idea, he would have to make her understand that. He watched her as she scraped the deer hide and prepared it. Sitting up on the side of the cot he caught Tahou's attention for a moment but quickly she averted her eyes so not to make contact with his. Clede reached over and grabbed the crutch Keewatin made from a tree limb leaning against the wall. Standing up and putting the crutch under his arm he limped over to the door then unlocked it and pulled it open. The cold air rushed into his face from outside; it was refreshing after being cooped up in the cabin for so long. He glanced out across the lake that was only partially frozen now. Only three inches of snow lay on the ground and the days were getting longer—summer was on its way. He watched as an eagle swooped down on the unfrozen portion of the lake but missed its prey, his talons came up empty. The bird circled a couple of times then disappeared over the forest. Turning around he pulled the door closed and locked it and returned to the chair by the table where he sat down. Clede noticed his bottle sitting on the table—he had maybe half of it left. From now on he would use it only if he had to. Clede picked up a stick from the firewood and pulled his knife out and began to whittle on it. The two of them hardly acknowledged that the other was present.

Toward the end of the day as night began to fall across the little valley Tahou finished her chores and lay down on the Indian blanket near the fire. Soon she was sound asleep. Clede watched as her breasts rose and fell in rhythm to her breathing. His attention was only momentarily diverted when he heard a lonely wolf holler somewhere in the mountain range. *Tahou,* he thought, *a very nice name.* He wondered about her and what kind of life she had with the Yellowknifes as a slave. Keewatin seemed to be good enough to her, but it was obvious that she meant nothing more to him than if she were his dog or horse. He fought off sleep even though his weakened body cried for it. Pictures of the girl stabbing him in his sleep kept racing through his mind. Walking quietly around Tahou he picked up some wood from the pile and added it to the fire. She raised her head to see what he was doing then laid it on her folded arms and fell back asleep. Clede poured some of the water from the bag on the peg into his cup. Taking some of the water he threw it in his face trying to stay awake. He could hear the wind blowing outside and sleet hitting against the back wall. He had to get some sleep, his body demanded it, so he hobbled to the cot and sat on the side of it. Pulling his knife from the sheath he would place it across his chest just in case. Clede lay there for another hour fighting sleep as he watched the young Indian girl asleep on the floor. An ember popped in the fireplace, she stirred but slept on without concern. His eyelids were getting heavier by the minute, he slowly drifted off to sleep.

Once during the night a noise awoke him suddenly, and with knife in hand he looked wide-eyed across the cabin. Tahou still lay on the floor not moving. This was killing him—he would have to have a talk with her. He had to know what her intentions were and possibly he would turn her loose. She could be valuable for supplies but he was not willing to risk his life with her. He never approved of slavery. Besides, he planned on moving on as soon as the weather broke and his leg was healed. This female was sure complicating his life.

Chapter 5

A week had passed since the departure of Keewatin. Tahou hadn't cut his throat yet; in fact, she hadn't even tried, just continued her daily business. Each day Clede became stronger and stronger and was able to walk now with the use of the crutch. The temptation that the young girl represented made life difficult for him. Trying to stay busy he sharpened his knife several times but her presence was noticeable. Tahou was well developed for her age: firm breasts, strong legs and a proportional buttock. Struggling to keep her off his mind he made arrows for the quiver and bow that he constructed. Keewatin had stolen the other one but no problem, there was a forest full of them for the making. He used them primarily for fishing to save his powder and balls for more important hunts.

The skies cleared late and a beautiful orange hugged the horizon as the sun dropped. His nerves were on edge, he had to make a move. Grabbing her hand as Tahou attempted to pass by, he saw her expression change to both fear and surprise at his sudden move. Pointing to the chair he directed her to sit down. Tahou slowly backing to the chair sat down gently staring into his eyes. He could tell she was anxious not knowing what his intentions might be toward her. Using his poor sign language he began to try and converse with her. He told her this was not his idea and that she was no longer a slave. She was free to go or stay—whatever she wanted to do. Any man would be proud to have her as his woman but not against her wishes.

She watched his hands intently and showed no emotion, which frustrated Clede even more that he couldn't get her to understand. Shifting himself on the cot he tried again repeating also out loud, "You are free to go, you are not my slave." Then she signed to him if there was anything else? Dumbfounded he just stared at Tahou. Didn't she understand he was giving her back her freedom? Slowly Tahou stood up and returned to her chores. Pondering in his mind maybe there was some honor code where she would have to escape rather than be set free. He would devise a plan whereby she would be left alone and free to make her escape if that is what it would take.

He was feeling stronger every day; maybe tomorrow if the weather was good enough he would walk back into the forest and hunt. They could use some fresh meat, all that was left was dried. She interrupted him with a bowl of the last of the fresh meat and some maize cooked in water from her Na Hcleth bag. Clede thanked her and scooped up the bits of meat and corn in his spoon. A sound out on the lake attracted his attention. He got up from the table and opened the front door. In the twilight of the evening he could see a flock of Canadian geese landing on the lake. He watched as they swam together toward the lakeshore. *A goose would sure taste good,* he thought, as he closed the door.

Trying to be friendly he offered his cot to Tahou; he figured it would be a lot more comfortable than sleeping on the dirt floor. She shook her head no, which flustered him some. She was not accustomed to sleeping on anything other than the ground. Clede thought to himself how glad he would be when he was rid of this woman. Finishing up the last of his meal he placed the empty bowl and spoon on the table. Then he stoked the fire and added a few more logs. That should burn for quite a while before more wood would need to be added. Clede walked back to his cot and pulled off one boot when Tahou squatted down and pulled the other boot from his bad leg. He couldn't figure her out; he shook his head as she prepared herself for bedtime. Lying back on the bunk he closed his eyes and went to sleep. Tahou lay down next to the fire on the floor staring into the flames. She did not understand that this man was offering her freedom. Little did Clede realize that Tahou was considered an outcast in her village and would not be welcomed back again. She had to admit to herself that this man was better to her than any other man had ever been, even Keewatin. She would stay with him and see what would happen before she made her final decision.

The next day early in the morning he arose and ate the food Tahou prepared for him. Then he put on his coat, hat, powder horn, buckled on his pistol, and grabbed his crutch that he put under his left arm. Tahou watched him intently but did not say a word as he prepared for the hunt. Opening the door he could see it was overcast but not a bad day so far. A few ducks swam along the western shore of the lake. Glancing back he could see that Tahou was watching his every move. He nodded to her and closed the door behind him. As he made his way toward the forest he said under his breath, "Good-bye, lovely maiden, have a safe journey." Clede was positive she would be gone upon his return. Walking was slow and the leg still pained each time the muscle tightened. Each step he could feel the leg strengthening; however, the hunt would be good. As he entered the forest a few flurries began to fall from the sky. Looked like they might be in for some more snowfall; he would mark his trail so if his tracks were covered he could find his way back easy enough. He glanced back at the cabin and could see it was quiet, only the stream of smoke from the fire could be seen rising above the roof. He could almost feel Tahou's eyes watching him waiting till he was out of sight so she could make her getaway.

Leaving a few tracks in the shallow cover of snow he would follow this trail and find a good vantage point to hunt from. He froze when he saw something moving fast through the forest. Dropping his crutch to the ground he pulled the hammer back on his rifle and brought it up to his shoulder. It was a lynx chasing a rabbit that was running for its life. They ran across his path no more than twenty yards in front. Neither animal knew there was another soul in the forest as they scurried, the rabbit changing directions rapidly to throw the cat off. The rabbit made a mistake and the lynx trounced on him grabbing him behind the neck with his teeth. Squealing lightly the rabbit went limp as life left his body.

Clede gingerly bent over and picked up his crutch. The lynx saw him and grabbed his kill and quickly ran out of sight deeper into the forest.

Several hundred yards back into the forest Clede found what looked like a good place to sit and watch. Several trails converged below—he would have a good angle to see if anything came down the mountain. Clede leaned on his crutch and left leg while he brushed a clean spot away with his right boot. Laying his crutch down next to the tree he put his hand on the tree to help him descend and sit down by the tree. Keeping his leg as straight as possible he leaned back against the tree and grabbed his rifle that he had propped against the tree. He rubbed his left leg, which throbbed some, and beads of sweat covered his forehead although it was a cold day. Clede was still weak but the leg was healing well and he felt he was well able to take care of himself again. That was a close call—he should have been dead but fate had smiled on him and given him another chance. He'd learned a valuable lesson the hard way.

Reaching down he cupped a handful of snow in his left hand and rubbed it on his sweaty forehead. Then he scooped up a handful and ate some of it to quench his thirst. He figured Tahou was long gone by now; she probably took what was left of the jerky and headed northeast. Clede couldn't kid himself, down in his heart he felt a bit sad to think that she would be gone. Then he saw some movement on one of the trails below. Slowly he cocked the hammer back on his Hawkens lying across his lap. It was a doe and a half-grown yearling following her close behind. They moved slow, stopping to paw in the snow occasionally. Clede thought a moment; he better take the young one, he wasn't strong enough to carry the larger doe. Looking down the barrel and lining up the sights he aimed at the young deer's neck just below the ear. Taking a deep breath and letting it out slowly he squeezed the trigger. The Hawkens fired sending a cloud of smoke into the forest. The young deer collapsed in his tracks and the doe quickly scampered off to safety. Clede blew the remainder of the smoke out of the barrel of the rifle. Then taking the powder horn he reloaded the rifle watching the young deer all the while. Once the rifle was reloaded he leaned it against the tree then grabbed the crutch. One hand on the tree the other on the crutch he pulled himself up standing on his right leg. It smarted some getting up, but he managed stretching to get the stiffness out of his body. He took another glance at the deer; he was still lying just where he fell. Clede put the crutch under his left arm and with his rifle in the right he limped down the mountain to where the deer lay. He worked his way down to the sitting position next to the deer and laid his rifle and crutch by his left side. Pulling out the knife he gutted the animal—this would lighten the weight of the animal some. Cutting slits through the hind legs he slipped a rope through the holes. Then he tied the legs together, and with the other end of the rope in his teeth he grabbed his rifle and crutch and worked his way upright. He tied the rope around his waist; he would drag the animal back to the cabin. It took him most of the rest of the day dragging the animal and stopping to catch his breath.

As he came out of the forest on the edge of the lake he looked toward the cabin. It looked the same, with a little curl of smoke protruding up into the overcast skies. Out of breath he sat down on a log close to the bank of the lake. Just a few patches of ice left on the lake. A flock of ducks flew by when an eagle swooped down trying to catch one but they were too fast for him as they flew up. He watched as the ducks circled the lake then flew up over the cabin, the mountain, then out of sight as they headed north. The eagle flew to the edge of the lake where it landed in a tree. As soon as he was well enough he'd check and see if he could find his traps. So far he hadn't had much luck trapping anything. Revived he stood up and made his way toward the cabin dragging the deer behind. Only about another hundred yards and he'd be there. It began to snow heavier as he neared the cabin. He felt a slight chill—it would be good to warm up by the fire. Fresh venison would be on the menu tonight.

He pushed the door of the cabin and it swung open. Clede stood there for a moment to allow his eyes to adjust to the darkness in the cabin. Standing his rifle against the cabin door he untied the rope from around his waist and let it drop to the ground. He would skin the animal after he drank some water and rested a bit. Then his eyes saw her. Shocked he stood there in disbelief as Tahou walked past him holding out her hand asking for his knife. Pulling it from his sheath he handed it to her. She grabbed the deer and rolled him on his back and began to skin the animal. Clede watched her for a couple of minutes then went in and put up his coat, hat, powder horn and rifle on their pegs. He poured some water from the bag into his cup and sat down at the table, leaning the crutch against it. Clede rested himself for a few minutes, taking out his bandana and wiping the sweat from his forehead. Then he scooted the chair closer to the fire where he would warm himself.

Tahou continued skinning the deer until she was finished. She hung the hide on the wall to allow it to dry. She laid the carcass across several logs then she skillfully cut the deer into strips that she could hang on the poles in the storage room for jerky. A larger chunk of meat she threw over her shoulder as she carried the meat into the cabin. She made several trips until she had hung all the meat on the poles in the storage room. That one piece of meat she cut into smaller strips, which she roasted over the fire. Clede, frustrated, just watched her in disbelief. What was wrong with the woman, didn't she understand she was free to go? Tahou stopped for a moment and Clede motioned for her to bring his backpack, which she did. He took out a cloth and rammed the bore of his rifle to clean it. Then he sharpened his knife till he had a keen edge on it, replacing it in the sheath on his side.

Then Tahou came over and squatted down at his feet pulling his boots off and rubbed his cold feet to warm them. Her warm hands stirred him as she gently massaged his feet. She looked up into his eyes and said something to him in her native language. Clede just looked at her. He bent over and put his boots back on then opened the door of the cabin and went out. The ground was covered as a light gentle snow fell from the cloudy skies. Spring couldn't be far off, he thought, the storms were much weaker now and the days were getting longer also. Clede gathered up enough timber to construct another chair. He thought that with what daylight was left there should be enough time to finish his goal. He walked back into the cabin and got his ax as Tahou looked up to see what he was doing. Then he went back outside and sat down on a log and began to build another chair. He worked vigorously and in a couple of hours he had finished the chair. Grabbing the chair by the back and his ax he returned to the cabin locking the door behind himself. He set the chair next to the table and called Tahou to come. Pointing at the chair he motioned for her to sit down. Tahou obeyed him sitting down in the chair. Then she smiled her gratification to him. Clede felt good—that was the first sign of warmth that he had felt from her. Then she got up and brought the roasted venison to the table for them to eat. She placed several pieces of the venison strips in front of him. They sat across from each other at the table as they ate. Tahou spoke to him in her native tongue of Chipewyan but he shook his head that he did not understand. She pointed at him and said "Wah-nay-ah." She picked up a stick from the fire and drew on the dirt of the floor. He began to understand that she was giving him an Indian name. "Wings of Wind Eagle," that was what she was trying to say to him. Tahou told him in sign language that he was always watching the eagles flying on the lake.

Then she began to tell him her story. As he watched her hands intently she told him that as a very young girl she had been captured by the Yellowknifes. Her people were the Chipewyan, they lived northeast many moons' journey from here. Keewatin grabbed her and carried her away to his people. She said that life was very hard for a woman with her native people. Women did most of the chores and carried most of the village on their backs and used dogs to pull toboggans whenever they would move. Life was very hard among her people. To be taken as a slave was a great dishonor, plus her people believed that the shamans from other tribes could inflict disease and curses into her body that could affect her people should she go back. Her father and mother both were killed in the skirmish with the Yellowknifes. She pointed at the bread cakes on the table and said, "Bakwezhigan." Clede understood that to mean bread. He picked up a piece and tried one but hid his displeasure at the taste. Soon as Tahou got up to fill their cups with water he threw the cake into the fire. He preferred the venison. She returned sitting down again at the table. Tahou pointed at his spear and said, "Anit." He replied, "Spear." They spent the rest of the evening learning to communicate with each other.

Tahou got up and put more wood on the fire then returned to sit down again. Clede began to tell his story. He told her about how he came to this country from across the Great Salt Lake, when he was just a baby. A terrible sickness had killed both his parents. He told her about his travel west on the iron horse and how had he met Kiska, his Nootka friend who taught him his ways. He told her how their lives were very similar in that they both were alone. Clede explained how surprised he was that she was still here after his hunt. He told her that she could stay or go, that was her choice. Looking into her eyes he told her that he was glad she had decided to stay.

It was late and the weakness that he still felt in his body had taken its toll. Rubbing his leg he lay down on the floor next to the fire and fell asleep. He had only been asleep for a short period of time when he felt Tahou lie down beside him. Startled he reached out to touch her under the Indian blanket only to feel that she was totally naked. He rolled over and faced her looking into her eyes glistening from the light from the fire. She helped him undress and then as they lay close together she placed his hand on her breast. That night they both found something that was missing in their life. He found paradise in this remote part of the world where time meant little.

Suddenly he opened his eyes the next morning as if he had woken from a dream. As he reached his arm across the lump that lay next to him he realized it wasn't a dream but the warm sensual nude body of Tahou. A woman didn't fit into his plans but this young Indian girl had found a way to his heart. Tahou opened her dark brown eyes and smiled. She gently put her arms around his neck and pulled him down on top of her. He kissed her lips softly. What else could be greater in his life at that moment? He had found love in this young Indian girl, a beautiful secluded peaceful valley, and plenty of provisions to sustain them both. After making love again Tahou rose up and stoked the fire, adding wood, and soon the cabin was warm. He lay on the floor and watched her as she prepared breakfast for them.

Later after they finished their meal, Tahou came and braided his long red hair. She tied two eagle feathers to the braids with strips of leather cut from the deer hide, which she had in her Na Hcleth bag. Clede knew at that moment, as she braided his hair, he was in love with this Chipewyan girl. Although she was only sixteen years old she was far more mature than her years. And Tahou thought how lucky that fate had brought them together. With her people she would have been treated like one of the dogs, as the women were expected to carry the load when the village moved. Life could be very hard in a Chipewyan village that usually consisted of a small family group. This white man with the fiery red hair was good to her and she felt more like a woman than ever. She was truly free for the first time in her life and it felt good. She remembered her days with Keewatin, as well as how many times she thought of escape but had no place to go. Now she had a place and this was her place beside Wah-nay-ah. Fate had brought these two people together from totally different cultures to become as one. The beautiful sparkling clear lake hidden deep in this little valley was as if they were Adam and Eve in the Garden of Eden. They spent the rest of the day frolicking and playing, getting to know each other even better.

The days grew longer, the weather changed and began to be much warmer with more time to venture out. The ice that covered the lake melted and Wahnayah recovered his traps. He and Tahou spent many enjoyable hours along the lake fishing and frolicking like two bear cubs. She taught him how to make a net that was placed on a pole. This net could be lowered into the lake. Tahou saved the entrails along with some meat scraps that she put in a pocket in the center of the net. Fish would come to feed on the bait and then they could raise the net, trapping them. At times he would just sit and watch her as she struggled to grab the wiggling fish in the net. How funny she was at times, he thought. Once she became angry with him for laughing at her and threw a rock at him hitting him in the back. She weaved a basket from the reeds that grew plentiful along the lake's edge and used it to put the fish in. She painted the basket with beautiful designs from paint she made from crushed stones and berries from the forest. Together they prepared the fish for drying which they hung on poles near the outside cabin walls. Some of the fish Tahou saved—they would eat fresh-caught fish tonight. Other times they would search the forest for berries, nuts and roots that could be eaten alone or prepared with the meals for flavor. He killed a young doe and Tahou made him a Na Hcleth bag to take with him on hunting journeys. She decorated it beautifully with her traditional painting and added beads and small bird feathers. On hunts she taught him how accurate she could be throwing rocks when she killed a grouse with a well-aimed throw.

Wahnayah increased the size of the storage building to accommodate the two of them. Tahou watched and admired his strength as she watched his muscles ripple as he cut the logs for the building. She felt secure with this strong man to protect her. Together they rolled the logs into place and she filled the cracks with mud and straw between them. After three days of hard work they completed the outside of the building. They then moved inside where they made poles for hanging meat and hides to dry. They would stay in the valley; this would be their home. Standing together closely with arms around each other they admired their accomplishments.

The valley was alive with beautifully blooming wild flowers. The work completed and plenty of food on hand, they would spend time swimming in the cold water of the lake. There were times when they would make love on the bank of the river then lie together naked under the warm summer sun. Other times they would stroll the bank of the lake picking up mussels and small shells to be used for decorations on clothes and making necklaces. Tahou taught Wahnayah to speak her language and he taught her some of his language. They spent hours talking, sometimes sitting to watch the eagles that swooped down sometimes successfully catching a large fish in its talons. They would fly to the nest they constructed in a large dead tree at the forest edge. Tahou taught him to play Chipewyan games and they would spend hours playing. Wahnayah always kept his Hawkens close at hand, even though they seemed totally alone; he remembered how Keewatin had stumbled on to his cabin that day. Even though this valley seemed totally secluded he knew not to let his guard down again.

Late that day they ate fresh fish with berries and nuts and then lay on the floor together watching the flames dance in the fireplace. Wahnayah felt the necklace she made for him earlier that day. She found an eagle dead at the lake's edge. Praying over the bird she plucked many feathers and then cut off the feet. She made Wahnayah a necklace with the talons, beads and small colorful smooth stones she found in the creek by the forest. Quietly snuggled together they fell asleep on the floor in each other's arms.

One day as they went about their chores Wahnayah noticed that Tahou was very quiet, she had hardly said anything to him all morning. This bothered him, he wondered if she were angry with him or perhaps she was not feeling well. She didn't act as if she were ill, maybe he was just imagining things. He turned back to rubbing bear grease on his badly worn boots. Tahou motioned for him to come but he ignored her as though he hadn't noticed. Angry she yelled at him "Omaa!" which meant come here. Smiling he turned facing her, then she also knew he was teasing her. Her smile turned to one of seriousness; he knew something important was weighing on her mind. Sitting down next to her he listened as she explained what was wrong. What she was telling him hit him like a bolt of lightning. She was explaining to him that she was pregnant with his child. For a moment he stood with a blank look on his face, which concerned Tahou, then he began to smile and holler, he was going to be a father. He grabbed her up in his arms and hugged and kissed her laughing with joy. She giggled with delight to see how pleased he was. Then his mind raced with thoughts, he would have to hunt more, build a baby crib. Gently he let her go, he didn't want to hurt her in any way. Tahou laughed at him, this silly big man. Placing her hand over his mouth to shut him up, she said with a smile, "Baby only eat doodooshaboo (milk) from my breast." Grabbing his hand she pulled him down as they both squatted down to their knees on the floor. Then Tahou began to chant as she thanked the Great Spirit for his many blessings on these two. He had to admit things had never been better in his life. After their prayer they walked to the door and looked out as the sky glowed a beautiful orange as the sun set in the west.

The wound to his left leg was completely healed with just a nasty scar left to remind him of the error he had made. He would hunt again in the same area where the buck had gored him in the leg. Hugging Tahou he grabbed his Hawkens and left the cabin and headed for the forest. Following the creek he came upon a place where beavers had partially dammed the waterway. This would be where he would set his traps in the future. There were many deer tracks in this area. Finding a good place to sit and watch he sat down and laid his rifle across his lap. He hadn't been sitting there long when he saw a large buck following a doe coming down the trail toward the water. Slowly bringing the Hawkens to his shoulder he took a bead and squeezed the trigger. The buck spun around and fell in his tracks. The doe scampered off into the forest at a dead run. Getting to his knees he reloaded the rifle as he watched to see if the deer would try to get up. He saw no movement and slowly he walked toward the buck. Checking the position where the animal lay he made a large circle around and came up to the deer's rear. He wouldn't make the same mistake twice. Coming near he kicked the large buck in the rear; he was dead for sure. He pulled out his knife and proceeded to gut the buck then he tied the horns and drug him down the hill toward the cabin.

As he came near to the cabin Tahou ran out and helped him pull the deer the remainder of the way. He threw a rope over a pole used to dry the meat and pulled him up headfirst. Tahou took over from here and skinned the animal. Wahnayah sat down and watched her. When finished she handed the hide to him. He scraped the hide while Tahou cut the deer up and hung the strips of meat on the poles. Tahou noticed how ragged his buckskins were; she would make him some new ones from the buck hide. She wanted her man to be handsome and dressed well, how proud of him she was. Yes, she would do her best work on a new set of clothes for him.

Several days passed and Tahou spent all her time working on his buckskins. She would wait till he left to go and check his traps on the beaver dam in the forest. Tahou could visualize his face when she handed him the new buckskins decorated in her native art. Wahnayah returned from the forest with a smile on his face—he finally caught two beavers in his traps. They would be something he could trade for at the trading post. Tahou skinned the beavers and then prepared the hides. He sat down at the table to sharpen his knife when Tahou snuck up behind him. She tapped him on the shoulder, and he turned in his chair and looked as she presented him with his new buckskins. Wow, he thought, they were really nice with fringe and plenty of color. They were almost too nice to wear—skillfully made and beautifully designed. Standing up he undressed quickly as Tahou impatiently waited on him. Slipping into the pants then putting the top on he stood before her with a big smile on his face. They fit perfectly. Hugging her and kissing her he said, "Thank you, I will be the envy of all women." Tahou laughed with delight. She would make him some knee-high moccasins next.

Wahnayah checked his backpack and noticed he was getting low on powder and balls. He decided he would use the bow and arrow whenever possible to save his ammunition till he could make it to a trading post. He was getting pretty good with the bow and arrow but the primitive weapon lacked the range his Hawkens had. He had done well trapping since moving to the dam on the creek. With Tahou's help he was getting the knack of it now and the storeroom had plenty of beaver pelts to trade. Together he and Tahou made plenty of arrows for his quiver at night before bedtime. She painted them with her traditional tribal colors and gave Wahnayah his own distinct markings. The arrows would be quiet killers—this he preferred to avoid attracting attention to their little Eden. Now he had to protect not only Tahou but also the new addition to their family.

Wahnayah discussed with Tahou that he needed to make a canoe to transport his furs to the trading post. He had watched the Nootkas many times as they built their canoes. Few could match their skill—he hadn't actually built one but believed he could do it. The next morning as the sun peered over the horizon in the east they were already busy preparing the day. Wahnayah found a large tree that would be just what he wanted to construct the canoe. The tree was just behind the cabin; he would cut it so it would drop into the clearing. He worked hard, stopping occasionally when Tahou brought water to him. It took him several hours to drop the tree and trim the roughage. Wahnayah began the painstaking chore of carefully hollowing out the canoe from the red cedar tree. One finger thickness at the top edges and two finger thicknesses at the bottom—these were the dimensions that Kiska had used. Tahou started a large fire which they placed rocks into to heat. Once the canoe began to take shape they put wood thwarts inside and filled it with water. Then they rolled red-hot rocks into the canoe and brought the water to a boil. After three days the canoe began to take shape. Wahnayah made a stern piece and hammered it into place using wooden pegs. Tahou helped him mold the stern into the figure of an eagle's head. Finally, after a week the canoe was complete. Wahnayah and Tahou drug the canoe to the bank of the lake. Pushing it out into the lake he paddled it out then back; he noticed no leaks. He was proud of his and Tahou's accomplishment. It would take them up the river to the trading post that Tahou told him about. Tomorrow they would load the furs for their trip.

Early the next day they loaded the canoe with the furs. They extinguished the fire then Tahou packed plenty of jerky and water for the trip. Tahou would ride in the front and he would take the back. They would take their time; Tahou estimated it would take them about a week to make the round trip. Tahou got in the canoe and Wahnayah pushed it out into the lake then they paddled to the mouth of the river and started the trip. They would follow the Quesnel River to Clarke's Trading Post—the Indians called it Pyna-tee-mooz. They paddled slowly on the river. Once they saw a large grizzly bear fishing for salmon in the river. He looked up but was not interested in anything but the numerous fish that swam by his paws. They moved on paddling all day till late in the evening, when they pulled into the bank and set up camp for the night. Tahou was sturdy, she never complained once to him that she was tired; in fact, she seemed to enjoy the trip. It felt good to bed down for the night. The canoe performed beautifully although it had many mistakes in it that the Nootkas would never accept. But they used theirs to hunt whales in the open sea and he had no intentions of taking on the Pacific.

Four days they paddled then around noontime they rounded a bend in the river and up above was the trading post. Not much to look at, a shabby large cabin that seemed out of place. They slid the canoe onto the bank then Wahnayah got out and grabbed the bow, pulling it well out of the water. He helped Tahou from the canoe; she stretched from the long hours of squatting while paddling the boat. With his rifle in his right hand he grabbed the cord that bound the furs together and lifting them onto his left shoulder he made his way to the building. Tahou followed close behind him. She opened the door for him as they entered the cabin. The place was cluttered with merchandise. A dark-skinned man grabbed his furs and helped him; he looked like a half-breed to Wahnayah. The man introduced himself as Jeremiah Clarke. Wahnayah answered him saying "My name is Clede."

"What can I do for you?" the man replied.

Clede said, "I need powder, balls, and caps for my Hawkens, and we need salt and flour." He noticed Tahou looking at an Indian blanket. He told Clarke, "And we'd like that Indian blanket.

Clarke replied, "Your woman, she be Chipewyan; don't see many this far south. They are a rugged bunch." Clede just stared at him and Clarke quickly averted his eyes returning to fill the order.

Two other Indians entered the trading post but Wahnayah didn't recognize them. Tahou whispered they were Blackfoot then she stood in the corner behind Wahnayah. He didn't like the looks of the people in the trading post, and as soon as Clarke had what he wanted he said to Tahou, "Maajaan," which meant go.

Tahou took the lead and placed the blanket in the middle of the canoe. Then she climbed in the front and sat down picking up her paddle. Wahnayah dropped his backpack in the canoe just behind the Indian blanket so if he had to he could get to it quickly. Hesitating for a moment he looked back at the trading post but no one was in sight. Shoving the canoe into the river he jumped in and took his position at the rear, laying his rifle next to his backpack. It should be faster moving on the way home, they would be going downriver. They paddled for several hundred yards then he pulled the canoe behind a large rock on the bank. Wahnayah didn't trust anyone since the incident back in Alki Point and the one with the Frenchmen. They sat chewing on some jerky for about an hour, and when he was sure no one was following then they moved out into the center of the river and headed home.

He was right, it only took them three and a half days to reach the point where the river branched into the lake. As they paddled toward the cabin it looked the same as when they left it. It was good to be back home. Wahnayah had plenty of supplies that should last him for a year or so before he would have to make another trip to the trading post. The baby should be old enough by then to travel with them. As the canoe slid up on the bank, Tahou jumped out but he shouted, "Omaa!" Tahou stopped and he motioned for her to stay by the canoe. Standing there he surveyed the area but saw nothing to indicate anyone had visited the valley while they were away. Slowly with his rifle ready and the hammer back he approached the cabin. Quietly he walked all the way around the building but saw no tracks or any signs. Then he kicked the front door open and it swung back. He stood there for a moment then entered the cabin. His eyes looked the room over but everything was just as they left it. Satisfied no one had invaded his or her domain he yelled for Tahou to come.

She ran and joined him in the cabin setting the Indian blanket on the table. Wahnayah returned to the canoe and unloaded it bringing everything into the cabin. Then he returned to the canoe and drug it up far onto the lake bank. It was late in the day and both were tired from the long journey. Closing and securing the door he noticed Tahou already had the fire going. He put away stuff; taking the extra gunpowder, he wrapped it in an animal hide and tucked it under his cot. He didn't want the powder to get wet or set it too close to the fire. Tahou unfolded the blanket and showed it to Wahnayah. He smiled and nodded it was very beautiful. She folded the old blanket up and placed the new one on the floor near the fireplace. The salt and flour he put in the storage room—he was damn tired of those cakes Tahou made. Maybe he could persuade her to use the flour mixed with grease, he figured that would taste a lot better. They went to bed early; it had been a long day. She undressed and invited him to lie with her on the new blanket. Even though he was tired he couldn't pass up Tahou's offer.

Tahou was beginning to show signs of a child, she was about four months pregnant now. Once she yelled for him to come as she felt the slightest tap of movement inside. Wahnayah felt her but he did not feel anything. He noticed that she had put on some extra weight since she had been pregnant.

He spent his days fishing or hunting, preparing for the winter. They had fresh fish or wild game daily now. His skill with the bow was improving each time he hunted with it. The Hawkens he used only when he killed larger game. He made a sling for the rifle so he could slip it over his head and carry it on his back. Other times he would follow Tahou into the forests as she searched for berries and roots; he felt he needed to protect her at all times. Occasionally he would help her pick the berries but mostly he would stand watch; his memory of the characters he saw at Clarke's Trading Post stuck in his mind. As he sat on the edge of the lake he watched a flock of geese that had taken up housekeeping along the bank of the lake. He laughed as he watched the babies struggle to keep pace with mother as she swam in search of food for the hungry brood. He watched as an eagle circled high above; the mother squawked and all her young scurried quickly to hide under momma's wings. If given half a chance the eagle would swoop down and grab one of the young, they would be easy prey for him. The valley was alive with regeneration of new life—how different it would look when winter came. His eye caught the splash of a fish near the bank, and standing up slowly with his spear in his hand he walked to the edge. A large pike was on the hunt but little did he know he was also being hunted. A quick flip of the wrist and his spear pinned the fish to the bottom. Grabbing the fish in the gills with his right hand he slung him onto the beach. Quickly he followed the wiggling fish then holding him down he gutted and cleaned the fish. This would be their meal tonight.

The summer went by quickly and Tahou became fussy as she began to increase in size from child. She noticed a restlessness in Wahnayah—he would spend hours just staring across the lake. They needed some time to be away from each other, she thought. The storeroom had ample supply of meat and there was more than enough firewood. There was very little left to be done and she spent time weaving a baby blanket. She knew in her heart what was bothering him. He needed to get away for a day or so on his own to think things out. Men were like this sometimes and she remembered how he had told her of his plans to one day travel to the other side of the lake. It was just something he was curious to investigate, and he wondered if there were any people living on the other side.

There he was standing at the doorway staring across the lake. She needed him close but that would be later. Walking up behind him she put her arms around his waist. She turned him around and looked into his eyes and told him, "You go. I am still seven or eight weeks from delivering the baby."

He replied, "But I do not want to leave you."

"I will be OK," she said.

He nodded. It would only be for a couple of days—the journey across the lake couldn't take more than a day and a half. He would make sure she had everything she needed so she would not have to venture out. "I'll leave my pistol in case you should need it." Sitting at the table he showed her how to pull the hammer back and then they went outside and he let her fire it once. She hit a log in the middle at twenty feet—that was good enough from anywhere in the cabin. He showed her how to reload it although he doubted she would remember how to do that. Wahnayah sat down with her and explained his plan: He could travel by moonlight and be home in about three days. She told him that she felt well, it was just the waiting for the baby to come out that was hard. He carried plenty of firewood inside and stacked it against the far wall. Then he filled the water bags with water so she would not have to leave the cabin for anything. Tahou prepared his Na Hcleth bag with plenty of jerky and berries, that would hold him till his return. He would take his Hawkens and bow with about a dozen arrows.

They spent the rest of the day just enjoying each other; he would leave in the morning at first light. A light mist fell as a few clouds quickly moved over the valley. It left a fresh clean smell to the land. Wahnayah was anxious to get started; he would feel better if he knew that as far as he could see they were alone. This would be the first time they had been apart since that first time he opened his eyes as she tended to his wound. It was good she was here and that he was not alone. Tahou reached out and grabbed his hand and quickly placed it on her abdomen. He felt it that time—the baby booted him in the hand. Wahnayah laughed, "He's a strong one, isn't he?"

Tahou smiled. "It may not be a son—would you be so disappointed?"

"No," he replied.

After they ate neither said anything. They just sat staring into the fire. He was already missing her, but he knew and she knew the time away would be good for both of them. He could hear the dripping of water as it showered outside and he hoped it would be gone by the time he headed out tomorrow. As they lay clutching each other Tahou whispered in his ear, "Don't stay away too long. The baby is restless to see his father." He pulled her tight as they fell asleep.

Chapter 6

The night was a restless one for Tahou but she knew that she had to let him go. As she opened the door to the cabin she looked to the east. A streak of brilliant orange with a soft blue background covered the sky. A light cool breeze brushed against the soft skin of her face as it blew from across the emerald lake. Wahnayah was up before she was, and she watched him drag the canoe down to the water's edge. Returning to the cabin he patted her on the stomach as he entered the cabin. Gathering up his gear that lay on the table he returned to the canoe placing it in the center. On his way back Tahou handed him a piece of deer jerky that he placed in his mouth as he went busily about his business. She closed the door and then stoked the fire as she thought how lonely it would be without him. But he was so anxious. It was a trip that he had wanted to take for a long time and it would be good for both of them, she thought.

He grabbed his rifle, checked the pistol and laid it on the table for Tahou should she need it. Then he grabbed her hand and pulled her up close to him as he hugged and kissed her good-bye. He promised her he would be back in a few days, and told her to keep the door locked and stay inside. She assured him that she would be making clothes for the coming baby. Then he picked up his backpack, turned and opened the door, and walked down to the canoe, laying the rifle on the backpack. With a hard shove the canoe moved out into the lake and with a final push he jumped in and sat down. He allowed the canoe to drift a ways into the lake before bending over and grabbing the paddle. Wahnayah took one last look toward the cabin and he could see Tahou waving at him from the door. He waved back, turned the canoe and began to paddle for the far shore. With slow hard strokes the canoe cut the water like a knife and he fell into a steady rhythm of rowing. Several hundred yards out in the lake he made one last glance over his shoulder; he could see Tahou turn and close the door to the cabin. A whisper on her lips to the Great Spirit, she prayed he would have a safe journey and come back to her soon.

Paddling steadily he felt a bit of guilt for leaving Tahou alone but assured himself she would be safe. He and Tahou had shared the cabin and valley for nearly a year now. The only humans he had seen the whole time he had been there were Tahou and Keewatin. Besides, Tahou had the pistol and he had taught her to handle and shoot it well. Lifting the paddle and quietly dipping it into the water then a hard push twisting it slightly in his hand when he lifted it from the water. The canoe barely made a wake as it slipped through the water as smooth as if he were floating on air. He would follow the bank around to the other side, staying out about fifty yards. He didn't want any surprises coming from out of the forest suddenly. Just out of reach of an arrow should someone decide to ambush him.

As he moved along he noticed many different animals coming to the lake to drink the water. A large bull elk looked up and watched him for several seconds then dropped his head and continued to drink, assured Wahnayah was no threat to him. Once a flock of ducks flew low over the top of him; he could hear their wings as they quickly cut the air, then they landed just off the bank near some reeds. A wolf stood on a rock watching as he passed by never moving a muscle. He glanced back and the wolf was gone as if he had suddenly disappeared into thin air. The sense of adventure returned to him as he again yearned to see what was ahead. The days were about equal to the nights now, he would move on until it was just twilight before setting up camp.

As the sun began to drop behind the tall forest he could feel the tightness in his arms as they ached from the long hours of paddling.

Moving closer to the shoreline he watched for a good place to pull in and camp for the night. Then his eyes caught sight of a small clearing where a creek flowed into the lake. Turning the bow of the canoe toward the shore he paddled hard toward the creek. As the canoe slid hard upon the sandy bank he grabbed his rifle and sat quietly for a few moments. Satisfied, he got up and stepped into the shallow icy waters. Walking forward he grabbed the bow and pulled the canoe way up on the bank. It had been a long day, he was tired and eager to set up camp and rest for the night. He noticed the creek had eroded out a deep crevice in the ground as it flowed into the lake. This would be good, he would camp on the side of the creek, which would hide his campfire.

As he unloaded his canoe he heard an owl hoot far back in the forest. Walking to a flat piece of ground near the creek he decided this was where he would make camp. With what little light remained in the day he quickly gathered up dead wood that lay in the forest. Soon he had a nice campfire burning and he unpacked his bedroll and laid it out. As he lay by the fire he chewed on some of the jerky Tahou had packed for him. He wondered if Tahou were missing him; this was the first night they had been away from each other since she first came into his life. Getting up he walked to the canoe and pulled it up far enough into the crevice so that no one on the lake could see it. Glancing across the lake toward the cabin he strained his eyes but could see nothing from this distance. Then he bent over and cupped some of the icy water of the creek and drank his fill. Going back to his blanket he sat down on the ground laying his rifle next to him. One thing he had learned, he'd make sure he didn't let his fire go out. He threw another log into the fire and watched as the embers floated up above the flames then went out. That night with the grizzly bear was an encounter he didn't want to repeat. Also some Indian tribes didn't take kindly to you coming into their area without permission. This would not be a restful night for sure and he wanted to be on the lake moving at daybreak. He slapped his neck as a mosquito sucked his blood, remembering Kiska's advice he returned to the creek bank and scraped up some mud, spreading it on his face, neck and back of his hands to ward off the pesky varmints. Then he returned to his bedroll and lay down. Putting his rifle on his chest he stared into the starlit night. He wondered if Tahou was thinking about him right now. He missed her warmth lying next to him. Bringing her along would have been his preference but she was in no condition to be traveling. As he dozed off his mind was full of the times they frolicked along the lake taking swims then lying naked together to dry.

Tahou sadly watched from the cabin door as the canoe slowly got smaller and smaller till she could no longer see it. She was missing him and he'd only just got out of her sight. Stay busy, that's what she told herself, and the time would pass quickly. Men sometimes needed time to themselves, she couldn't understand it but she knew this. No time to feel sorry for herself, she had a baby to get ready for. She rubbed her stomach as the child inside kicked her hard. She chuckled to herself, "I know you want to come out but it is not time yet. Besides, you must wait for your father to return." What a good man he was; she had grown to love her Wahnayah. She remembered how bad she felt when she learned that Keewatin would give her away. She was glad about her decision to stay that morning when he went out to hunt. She knew he was giving her an opportunity to leave but she had no place to go. How happy she was for the first time in her life.

It seemed like an eternity to her without Wahnayah at her side. Rising up early the next day she strained her eyes but knew he wouldn't be coming back this soon. Just another day or so and she would expect to see him paddling hard to get back to her. She could just feel him wrapping his muscular arms around her and his warm lips against hers. Closing the door she decided to work on the bearskin coat she had been preparing for him. She hid it in the storeroom so that he would not know what she was doing. It would be a great gift, she could just see his face when she presented it to him.

It was a warm day and she was hot from the child. She climbed the ladder and opened the trap door on the roof. Sitting at the table she worked softening the bearskin. Lost in her thoughts and preoccupied with her work she hadn't heard the approach of a stranger at the cabin door. Outside they surrounded the cabin; there were six of them, renegades that were outcasts from their own tribe. They had banded together like a pack of wild dogs looking to kill, rape, and steal from whomever crossed their path. The leader of the group was approximately thirty-five years old and had a bad scar across the crown of his nose. The scar came from a tomahawk in the face while fighting with his brother that came very close to ending his life.

The lowly group had been following the lake when they accidentally came upon this cabin hidden near the tree line. They probably would have missed it altogether but the curl of smoke caught Nishkaadizi maiingan, or Angry Wolf's, eye. Watching from the forest for many hours they studied the cabin but hadn't seen anyone. The renegade leader Angry Wolf decided it was easy prey and decided to approach the cabin. He made his way to the front door and gently tried it but could tell it was locked from inside. Motioning for the others they joined him by surrounding the cabin.

Mikinaak came in from the back of the cabin and crawled upon the roof when he noticed the open trap door. Little did Tahou know that opening the trap door had been a grave mistake on her part. Mikinaak with knife drawn peered down the opening and could see the young woman sitting at the table. He slowly bent over and looked into the room and could see she was alone. Quietly he stepped on the first ladder rung then dropped to the floor in the middle of the room. Tahou, startled, reached for the pistol but she was too slow. Mikinaak grabbed the pistol and backhanded her hard, knocking her to the floor. Stunned, Tahou lay still as Mikinaak opened the front door and waved for the others to join him. Tahou struggled to clear her head and to regain her footing but Angry Wolf grabbed her by the hair and jerked her head back putting a knife to her throat. She tried with all her strength to fight him off but in her condition he was much too strong for her. She begged them not to hurt her because she was with child but the words fell on deaf ears. Angry Wolf took his knife and slit her buckskins down the back and tore her clothes from her body. Then he threw her to the floor. She cried in agony as she started into labor but nothing phased these animals as they took turns raping her. Once through with her Angry Wolf pulled her head back and cut her throat, throwing her lifeless body into the corner of the cabin.

Laughing he licked her blood from his arms then he ransacked the cabin along with the others looking for anything worth stealing. Tahou lay motionless, her life's blood soaking the dirt floor under her naked bruised body. Pulling his knife from its sheath he returned to where Tahou lie. Bending over he cut her right breast off then scraped the inside as if he were cleaning an animal hide. Milk for her unborn baby mingled with blood flowed across her chest and dripped to the floor. He would use her breast to make himself a bag to carry his tobacco. Mikinaak tried to hide the pistol from Angry Wolf but he grabbed him and jerked the pistol from his pants. Pointing the weapon at Mikinaak he pulled the trigger back and at the last second turned and fired the bullet into Tahou's body. "You trying to steal from me, Mikinaak?" Then the others ducked and scrambled as he waved the pistol around the room in evil glee. Then he let the hammer down and put a leather cord through the trigger guard and tied the ends together. Next he slipped the strap over his head he let it dangle from his chest. Slowly the others came out of their hiding places as he went back to searching the cabin. When he was convinced they had taken everything of value Angry Wolf motioned for the others to follow as they left the cabin. They moved back into the forest; they would camp there tonight and watch to see if her man returned. If no one showed they would move on.

Sitting up suddenly it took a moment for him to realize where he was and remember that he was not at home in the cabin. A light mist fell and he could hear as the drops of water made a noise as they crashed to the forest floor. Glancing at his fire he could see it was still burning low. He bent down and scooped up dirt throwing it onto the fire and extinguishing it. Scattering the stones he tried to cover up any sign that someone had spent the night there. He pulled open the flap on his Na Hcleth bag and took out a piece of jerky and chewed on it as he rolled up his blanket and tied it. Then he slung the backpack over his left arm and with his rifle in his right he walked to the canoe. Setting his stuff in the center he pulled it down to the lake bank. He took one good look across the lake then up and down the bank but he could see nothing. Shoving the canoe hard into the lake he jumped in grabbing his paddle. Sitting down and making himself comfortable he began to oar out into the lake. He rowed out then turned the bow toward the far bank, which he could probably reach by noon. Wahnayah was feeling guilty for leaving her alone, he was anxious to head home.

As the canoe slid upon the sandy bank he set the paddle down and picked up his rifle cocking the hammer. He sat quietly surveying the area. A hawk screeched as it flew into the forest on the hunt. Several minutes passed and then he stood up and stepped from the canoe. He bent over and picked up his pack slipping it onto his back. Grabbing the bow of the canoe he pulled it far upon the bank out of sight. Letting the hammer quietly down on his Hawkens he pulled his knife from the sheath. Cutting foliage from the nearby brush he covered up the canoe. He would scout the shoreline then go inland several hundred yards looking for any signs of humans. The forest was thick with tall fir trees. Quietly and cautiously he stepped into the edge of the forest taking a few steps and stopping then moving on. He spotted a trail that led through the forest, he would follow it for a ways. Something through the trees caught his eye, a clearing about fifty yards back in the forest, which was unusual. Stooping down behind a nearby tree he sat there studying what appeared to be a rather large structure. It was a longhouse similar to the one the Nootkas lived in. Pulling the hammer back on his rifle he moved a little closer. A tall totem pole stood out front near the entrance to the building. The totem pole had the head of an eagle carved on the top. It stood about forty feet high facing the lake as though it was there to protect. He dropped down in the prone position and lay there for nearly an hour watching for any sign of life. No smoke came from the building—it appeared to him that it was deserted, but why? Slowly getting to his feet he took another look around in all directions but saw and heard nothing. Slowly he worked his way completely around the structure staying back in the trees for cover. Crouching down he came in from the rear of the building and slowly walked along the wall with his rifle cocked. Stopping he put his ear against the wall but heard nothing coming from inside. Coming around the corner of the building he hesitated then approached the doorway. Taking a deep breath he pushed his foot against the door and to his surprise it swung open easily.

Stepping into the doorway he hesitated a moment to let his eyes adjust to the darkness inside. A very heavy stench hit his nose causing him to gag. As his eyes adjusted to the darkness a horror struck him at what his eyes saw. He couldn't believe it—there were approximately twenty-five individuals scattered around in the building, all appeared to have been dead for at least a couple of days. Some were stacked in a pile near where the fire had once burned. He noticed two hanging from overhead. One hung upside down, a female she had one breast viciously removed; the other was a man hanging by the neck. The thing that horrified him was they were skinned like an animal. He wondered if they were skinned alive or whether they had been killed first. The sight was sickening to him. By the looks of the expressions on their faces he figured they must have been skinned alive. As he surveyed the carnage he could see some of them were young children, this made his anger boil. Some had even been dismembered, the body parts lay around on the floor. What kind of animals could do this to innocent women and children? Reaching up he cut the two hanging from the roof down and let them drop gently to the floor. Looking around he picked up blankets and whatever he could find to cover the bodies. He couldn't stand the smell any longer, he made his way through the door closing it shut behind him. Stooping down on one knee he noticed tracks in the dirt. He figured there were at least four, maybe more. A cold shiver went down his spine when he realized they headed north. Tahou and the cabin lay north and they had a head start on him.

Urgency filled him as he quickly maneuvered through the forest to the canoe. This group was dangerous to whoever came in contact with them. Forgetting about his own safety he could only think of the welfare of Tahou. Uncovering the canoe he threw his stuff in the center, and dragging it to the lake he pushed it into the water jumping in and grabbing the paddle. Visions of horror filled his mind as he dug the paddle in hard and rowed out into the lake. After oaring in a panic for about thirty minutes he realized he had to slow down some. No way he could keep up this pace. Slowing down to long, smooth rhythmical strokes he moved toward the far shore as the canoe slid through the clear water. His mind was full of pictures and the horrible smell from what he had just witnessed. As dark began to fall he pushed on even though his arms ached with pain until he realized it was just too dark to proceed. Running the canoe bow hard onto the bank it slid about halfway up. Sitting there with rifle next to his side he would just sleep in the canoe. As soon as there was enough light he would be moving on again anyway.

Bending down he opened the flap on his bag, reaching inside he grabbed a piece of jerky. Sitting in the dark he slowly chewed on the dried meat. It tasted good it had been a while since he had eaten anything. When he was through with the jerky he leaned over the side of the canoe and dipped up some water and drank it. It tasted good to his dry mouth, he was exhausted. It felt good to rest his arms. Picking up his rifle he laid it across his body and then lay back in the canoe. He was very tired but he just wasn't sleepy. As he looked up into the stars above a shooting star flashed across his vision. Damn, if it would have just been a moonlit night he would have kept moving. Common sense told him he had to rest or he wouldn't be worth anything by the time he reached home. He dozed off then woke again; he prayed that he would find Tahou safe. How foolish he had been to leave her alone. How was he to know danger was so close they had been lulled into a false sense of security?

Jerking awake suddenly the next morning he sat up in the canoe. He moaned from the soreness in his body, stretching, trying to loosen up. The hammer was back on his rifle, he must have pulled it back out of instinct when he awoke suddenly. Quietly he eased the hammer down on his Hawkens and relaxed for a few seconds. The canoe was sure not a comfortable place to sleep. He could see a hint of daylight breaking back in the east. Opening his bag he reached for a piece of jerky and chewed it until he had eaten it all. That would probably be the last he would eat today until he reached the cabin and was sure Tahou was safe. He waited about thirty minutes, by then enough light filled the sky that he could see to make his way. He stood up in the canoe and stretched his legs, it felt good. A shiver went down his back from the cool damp air. The temperature always seemed to get cooler right before daybreak. Glancing across the lake he could see that there was enough light now for him to see so that he could continue on. Stepping out of the canoe with both feet he grabbed the side of the canoe and pushed it back into the lake. Jumping into the canoe he moved his rifle to the center of the canoe and picked up the paddle. Making himself comfortable then he dug the oar into the water hard. Once again he picked up the smooth strokes as he oared hard for the far shore. Wahnayah strained his eyes to catch any sight of the cabin but he was just too far out. The sound of the water rippled past the bow of the canoe as it cut gently through the water. He only stopped once to drink some of the lake water and wipe the sweat from his forehead before resuming.

His body and arms ached and there was sweat dripping from his face as he strained his eyes to see the cabin on the distant shore. About midday was when he first spotted the cabin sitting at the base of the mountain nestled at the edge of the trees. Quicker and quicker came the strokes as he slapped the oar into the water and pushed hard. Panic began to fill him when he could not see any smoke drifting up above the roof of the cabin. His eyes frantically searched for any movement anywhere of Tahou but he saw nothing.

As he moved closer he was just offshore moving fast; he could see the cabin well now. His mouth parched with thirst but he wouldn't even stop to drink until he knew she was safe. Finally the canoe hit the shoreline hard and slid far up onto the sand. Even before it came to a complete stop he had already leaped from the canoe grabbing his rifle as his feet hit the sand. Quickly he cocked it on the run as he approached the door of the cabin. Wahnayah yelled her name out loud but there was no response from inside. Maybe she was asleep, maybe the baby had come early—his mind raced with speculation. As he neared the front door he noticed it was slightly ajar. A sick cold feeling came over him. He sensed something was not right. With his Hawkens in his right hand and ready for business he shoved the door open. It creaked lightly as it swung back. Again he yelled her name but he heard not a sound from within. From the door he could see the table was lying on the side. Wahnayah hesitated just for a second searching the room for any unusual forms. Then he moaned as tears filled his eyes when he saw Tahou lying face down by the far wall. Easing the hammer down on the rifle he propped it against the wall as he raced to her side. A large pool of blood covered the floor underneath her naked body. Gently he turned her over and nearly threw up when he saw how she was mutilated. Kicking violently at the chair near them he sent it flying across the room crashing into the far wall. Then he sat down next to Tahou on the floor and covered his head with his hands and cried loudly with despair. His heart burned with rage, he could think of nothing but to find out who did this and tear them apart. He sat grieving in the corner all night, he just couldn't accept the fact that she was gone. So many questions filled his mind—Why?

Sometime during the next morning he came to his senses. Picking up the crumpled blanket that he and Tahou had made love on many times, he noticed she had tried to deliver the child that was half out of her. Tears flowed down his cheeks as he gently pulled the baby boy from her body. Then he softly placed the baby in her arms. Throwing the blanket over them he rolled them up. Opening the end he reached in and cut several locks of her hair. Tying a string around the locks to hold the hair together he slipped them into his bag that hung on his side. This was all he had left of what was going to be a beautiful family. Stooping down he put his arms under the blanket, and lifting them both he then laid them on the floor in front of the fireplace. He remembered the many beautiful nights they fell asleep in each other's arms. There was nothing left inside, his only reason to exist was to find the ones who had done this and make those responsible pay for this hideous act.

He walked around the room looking for the pistol that he had left her. Searching in the storage room he found a pair of moccasins that Tahou made for him. They were hidden lying in between the pile of logs near the wall. They were beautiful; he touched the soft leather to his face and smelled the clean leather. He whispered under his breath, "Thank you, Tahou." Sitting down he took his old worn-out boots off and put on the knee-high moccasins, fit perfectly. The pistol was nowhere to be found, undoubtedly they had taken it with them. He wondered if Tahou had had a chance to even use it. Studying the footprints on the floor, it didn't look like it. The only blood that he could see visually was that of Tahou in the corner. Then he noticed the trap door was open. That must have been how they surprised her. He could tell by the moccasin prints on the floor—one set was deep, as though someone had dropped from the roof. This must be the same group of individuals responsible for the massacre in the village across the lake. The footprints told him that there were at least three of them, maybe more.

Packing his bag with all the supplies he could carry he set the buildings on fire. Sitting down on the ground outside he watched as it slowly burned. He watched as his world and his life drifted into the skies in the smoke. Burning with rage inside he vowed to Tahou that he would avenge her death he would not rest until he had hunted them down. Then the cabin moaned as it collapsed into a red-hot pile of burnt wood. Picking up his rifle at his side he walked down to the lake. Stooping to one knee he bent over and washed his face with the cold water, drinking some of it. Returning to the cabin he stood for a few minutes watching as the final few flames flickered from the heap of black ashes. Bending over he studied the tracks that told him they had headed toward the forest at the edge of the lake. Shaking his head he tried to clear his mind to what seemed like a terrible nightmare, thinking any moment he would awaken from a bad dream. Touching his knees with his hands as he studied the tracks, he realized it was no dream. How could such evil have invaded this beautiful valley that he and Tahou loved as their Eden? Then he lifted the heavy pack onto his back, and picking up his rifle he followed the tracks that led away from the cabin.

As he entered the forest he noticed a place where they had camped. Cold black ashes were all that was left of their fire. They must have waited around hoping to catch him return and finish the job. One mistake they made was not waiting long enough for his return; he hoped it would cost them their lives. As he followed the trail several times during the day he lost sight of it but would make a big circle until he picked up on it again. They were moving northwest, in the direction of the Rocky Mountains. The trail led him up and over a mountain. Stopping at the summit he stood for a long period of time searching for any movement below. A few drops of rain caught his attention as they hit him in the face. He could barely feel them he felt so numb. His attention back on the trail he moved on again his pace feverishly picked up. He caught himself—he'd better slow down, he wanted his revenge before they killed him.

Dropping off into the canyon then up the side of the next mountain, he stopped halfway up to catch his breath. A puff of wind blew the eagle feathers in his hair, they rested on his shoulder. He reached over and touched them as if he expected Tahou to grab his hand. It was late, darkness would be upon him soon as he reached the top of the saddle between two mountains. Wahnayah looked for a good place to bed down for the night. He was tired, he had pushed himself hard. He would slow down; it was apparent they had a pretty good head start on him. It would take days for him to catch up with them. As long as the trail was fresh he would find them. They were not hard to follow, they left a path of death and pain wherever they went. A large tree lay fallen on its side; he would set up camp next to it but there would be no fire. He guessed they were maybe two days ahead of him. Surprise was his only ally, they had him outnumbered but if he could catch them sleeping perhaps he could get them all. It didn't matter to him if they killed him, he just wanted to take the one out who cut Tahou's breast from her. He hoped she was dead when he did that to her.

Clearing a place on the ground with his moccasins he dropped the bag and sat down leaning his back against it. His rifle lay across his lap as he looked up at the partial moon as it came out from behind a cloud. There was enough twilight showing so he was able to see any movement coming through the forest. He would be hard to see with the fallen log shadowing him. He felt very tired physically and mentally; it had been tough the past two days. The wind blew across his face; it was getting cool he knew that winter would be coming in the near future. His rifle resting across his lap he slipped his finger on the trigger and placed his thumb on the hammer. Closing his eyes he laid his head back against the log.

The next morning he rose up early, sitting in the dark watching as daybreak slowly rose in the east. Soon it was light enough that he could pick up the trail again. He knew they couldn't be too far in front of him. As he followed the trail he came into a small clearing and spotted what was once a campfire. Stooping down he picked up some of the ashes in his left hand. They were still slightly warm. His heart beat faster, he was gaining on them. All he could see in his mind was Tahou's battered body lying on the floor of the cabin. Her life's blood soaked into the dirt on the floor. He would have to move a bit slower and more cautiously; his trigger finger was itchy but he must force himself to be patient. They were near, his chance would come.

Dumping the ashes from his hand he picked himself up and continued to trail them. The trail was too easy to follow; they were not aware they were now the hunted. As he reached the edge of the next mountain he looked in the canyon below and once he thought he saw movement in the trees below but couldn't be certain if it was human or animal. He thought about the eagles swooping down and digging their talons into an unexpected prey. Wahnayah wished he had that kind of power. Dropping off the mountain he cautiously made his way down the side of it. Stopping when he spotted a lone wolf coming out of the canyon. He watched as the wolf kept looking back as he moved on quickly. Something was in that canyon, perhaps who he was looking for. The wolf never knew Wahnayah was watching him. His attention was on whatever was down there. Once the wolf was out of his sight he moved on slowly.

By noon he reached the bottom of the canyon. Making his way through the thick forest he came across where they had stopped. He was very close, he knew that. They had stopped to rest near a creek, probably last night. Checking the ashes in their campfire, he found they were very hot and the embers were glowing red. Dropping to his knees he looked as far ahead as he could see through the forest but saw nothing. Studying the tracks he knew there were at least four of them. He sat there for maybe half an hour before he decided to move on. If he could catch up to them he figured he would make his move tonight or before daylight in the morning. Very cautiously he moved on, following the tracks until they turned following a well-defined trail between two mountains. It was nearly dark by the time he came into a flat stretch of ground with mountains on each side. A small trickle of a creek flowed nearby; he would camp here tonight and start early before daybreak. He figured he would come upon them just ahead and make his move before good light.

Walking over to the creek he bent down on one knee and cupped some of the water as he looked through the forest but there was no movement. He noticed his reflection in the creek, his long hair braided with two eagle feathers and the buckskins. He wondered what his father would think of him if he could see him now. There was a tree back in the forest away from the creek, this is where he would sit down and rest with his back against it. Anxiety filled him as he contemplated what his strategy would be for the following morning. They would be sleeping, not aware that someone was stalking them. He figured he could probably take two of them out before they would know what hit them. One with the Hawkens, the other he would cut his throat, a third maybe with the spear—he sat working on his plan in the dark. The rifle would then become his club—it didn't matter, he only knew he would kill as many as he could before they got him. It was time for him to make things right.

Chapter 7

The next morning he was suddenly awakened by the sound of someone walking toward him. Quickly he struggled to clear his eyes and scramble to his feet. He saw several dim forms moving in the dim light of the forest. Pulling the hammer back on his Hawkens quickly but then he felt a deep burning across his head as one of them hit him with a tomahawk from behind. Stunned for a moment he felt hands grab and hold him down then another blow between the shoulders as one of them ripped the rifle from his hand. Wahnayah fought to regain consciousness but the wind was knocked out of him when a fist hit him in the stomach. They were Indians, he knew that but he didn't recognize their markings and what tribe they were from. Attempting to push himself up by his arms as he was hit again knocking him down and out. He crumbled to the ground as the group stood over him arguing and fussing amongst themselves. Angry Wolf kicked him in the rib cage and spit on him. Mikinaak bend down and unbuckled his pants, pulling them off—they would be his. The group stripped Wahnayah down, leaving him bruised, whipped and naked. Then they drug him by his feet to a nearby tree and lashed him to it. Coming to momentarily, his head spinning and pain wracking his body, he could hear voices but couldn't understand the dialect. They weren't Chipewyan or Yellowknife, that was for sure. At that moment he figured he was going to die, then he slipped back into unconsciousness again.

It was dark when he came to again. He struggled to clear his head and remember what had happened to him. Where was he? He felt something wet in his eyes and he blinked, trying to clear them. Then he remembered the blow to his head, hearing voices then another blow and nothing but blackness. Every inch of his body hurt as he felt his hands tied tightly behind him around the tree. As his throbbing head began to slowly clear some he realized that he was naked. They had beaten him badly—the wetness in his eyes was his own blood that came from a gash in the side of his forehead. He could hear voices out about twenty feet in front of him. Raising his head just a little he looked through swollen eyes and could see a fire burning. There was a group of them huddled around it. A cool breeze blew over his naked body that caused a shiver to go up his spine. Pulling against the binds that held his hands he could feel they were very tight, they were cutting off the circulation. As he sat there in the dark he twisted and pulled against the rope and felt them loosen a little. It felt good—he could at least feel some of the circulation returning to his hands. The wetness he felt was probably his blood, he thought. Well, he was still alive for now—Why?—he couldn't answer that question. These cutthroats seemed to get pleasure from torturing their victims to death. These were the ones he had been trailing. As careful as he had been, they must have spotted him.

Running his tongue over his lips he used the blood dripping from his forehead to wet his dry mouth. Working his hands in the dark attempting to free himself, he watched as they passed a pipe around. They appeared to be drunk, to him, as they talked loud, laughing and joking. He could see a bottle; that had to be his scotch. No doubt he knew now these were the ones he was after. The scotch they were drinking alone couldn't have made them this drunk. There wasn't that much left in it, he recalled. The tobacco in the pipe they were smoking probably contained some drug in it. Then one of them got up and staggered away from the fire then fell to the ground passing out. He tried to count how many there were but it was difficult seeing them, his eyes were so swollen. The one with a face full of tattoos yelled something at the one passed out on the ground. Wahnayah heard him call him Mikinaak.

He pulled hard on his binds as the anger welled up in him. He could visualize this scum laying their hands on Tahou and raping her. The pain from his wrist brought him back to reality—he would have to slowly work himself free. If he were going to have any kind of chance he had to free himself. Then he felt the bindings slipping over his hands—the wetness was lubricating them. Wahnayah kept his head hanging low so as not to attract any attention to himself. Every once in a while one of them would glance his direction and he would act as if he were still unconscious. He noticed the one with the tattoos seemed to be the ringleader. Watching as he pulled out a pouch which held the tobacco, he noticed something strange about it. Then a cold chill of anger filled his whole body as he realized the pouch was made from a woman's breast. He remembered that one of Tahou's breasts had been cut from her body. Pulling as hard as he could against the bindings he felt one of his hands slowly slip loose. At last he was free but he would sit there as if he were still unconscious and tied up. He would bide his time and wait for the chance to make his move. Then revenge would be his on these damn savages. Puntahaw was what they called the one who had his knife. He was cutting off a piece of jerky from Wahnayah's bag.

It was late into the night by the time the group had either passed out or fallen asleep. Puntahaw was the only one still awake. He stumbled over to where Wahnayah sat with his head down. He kicked Wahnayah in the side. Gritting his teeth against the pain he made no sound, he just sat there as though he were still unconscious. Satisfied, the Indian made his way over to his blanket by the fire and joined the others as he too lay down. Wahnayah sat quietly against the tree; he would give them a couple of hours to be in a deep sleep before he would make his move.

Several hours had passed. It was time. Slowly he brought his hands from behind the tree. Reaching over he untied the rope from the other hand. He would save the leather rope, he could use it as a weapon if given the chance. Planning his next move he saw that one of them was lying further out away from the fire close to him. Very slowly he got down on all fours and crept toward him. He didn't want to awaken them, that would be his demise. Like a puma on the hunt he inched closer and closer toward his victim. As he neared one of them moaned and rolled over—Wahnayah froze for just a second then continued on. In the dim light of the smoldering fire he saw his rifle lying by the side of the sleeping man. It was about time that lady luck shined on him. Reaching over he very slowly lifted the rifle away from the sleeping man. Quietly he eased the hammer back. Then he slowly stood to his feet and lifting the rifle high above his head he slammed the butt into the man's forehead. He heard his skull crack like a ripe watermelon under the force of the thrust. The man kicked and went limp. Puntahaw lifted his head to see what was going on and Wahnayah turned his Hawkens on him pulling the trigger. He saw the bullet hit him in the forehead blowing the back of his head off. Then he jumped quickly into the center of the remaining three that lay around the fire. By this time they were all trying to clear their heads and get to their feet. He swung the Hawkens with all his might, hitting the one called Mikinaak between the eyes—the Indian dropped like a rock. Then he swung back the other way hitting another one on his temple, killing him instantly.

Angry Wolf dove into his chest with his knife drawn. Wahnayah fell backwards as they tumbled into the darkness. Wahnayah felt his wrist and grabbed his hand that held the knife as they rolled across the ground. Wahnayah rolled on top of Angry Wolf quickly putting a fist into his nose. He slammed his hand into a rock and felt the knife fall free. Angry Wolf shoved hard trying to knock Wahnayah off of him. But he was too heavy for him in his drunken state. Wahnayah found the knife in the dark then jabbed it into the shoulder of the Indian. He felt the knife plunge down to the hilt before stopping. Angry Wolf groaned as Wahnayah hit him hard in the face knocking him into unconsciousness. He felt him go limp underneath him. Jerking the knife out he reached down and grabbed him by the hair of the head and drug him to the same tree he had been tied to. Wahnayah cut the clothes from Angry Wolf's body till he lay naked on the ground. Then he tied his hands tight behind the tree with the same leather rope.

Walking back to the campfire he threw his clothes into it. They ignited the fire then he added wood to it till it was roaring high enough to cast light across the entire camp. Bending down he checked each of the renegades making sure they were dead. He picked up his pistol lying near Angry Wolf's pipe. Then he pulled his buckskins from Mikinaak's dead body. Slipping a leg into the pants he pulled them up and tied the leather ends that kept them tight around his waist. He felt the decorations on the shirt, he could almost feel Tahou's hands as they skillfully added the beads. Buckling the belt around his waist he returned the pistol to its place in the scabbard. Wahnayah took turns dragging each of the dead savages out of the camp and out of his sight. He wouldn't bother to bury them, they weren't worth any more of his time. Then he gingerly sat down near the fire and reloaded his Hawkens.

His eyes glanced toward Angry Wolf when he saw that he had regained consciousness. He got up, and leaving his rifle near the fire he circled the tree and checked the binds to make sure the scum hadn't tried to free himself. Wahnayah felt no remorse for killing this brood, they deserved far more than what he had done to them. Emptiness filled him as he realized he had avenged Tahou's death but even so that couldn't bring her back. Walking around the tree he stood there staring at the naked Angry Wolf and thought about what he could do with him. Clouds rolled in from the west and covered the sky, and as a light mist fell he turned and went back to the fire adding wood to it. Then he sat down and reached over and picked up the water bag that the renegades had stolen from his cabin. He poured some of the water into his hands and washed his face and the dried blood from the wound on the side of his head. He reminisced about the long swims he and Tahou made, her beautiful face smiling back at him.

Angry Wolf came to later in the afternoon, the light rain revived him. Looking at Wahnayah sitting by the fire he started chanting and yelling at Wahnayah in his native tongue. Then Wahnayah became enraged by the Indian's arrogance and pulled the pistol from the scabbard. Without thinking he fired a single shot at the Indian, hitting him in the groin and severing his testicles. Angry Wolf screamed in agony then crumpled forward against his binds. Wahnayah raced over to where the Indian was tied. He started to hit him with the butt of the pistol but he could see he was dead. *Just as well,* he thought, *you got far less than what you deserved.*

Pulling his knife out he reached behind the tree and cut the binds. Angry Wolf fell forward lying face down on the ground. Wahnayah grabbed his feet and drug him to where the others lay outside of the camp. Then he whispered under his breath, "Now you can spend eternity in hell together."

Wahnayah returned to the campsite and built a lean-to, to protect him from the rain. He ate some of the jerky that was in his bag then he lay down and curled up near the fire. His body was still very sore from the many bruises and cuts he had obtained at the hands of this band. His pistol in his hand and his finger in the trigger he fell asleep, he needed the rest. Last night had been very difficult, he came very close to death again. They should have killed him when they had the chance but in their sick minds they thought they had to torture him to death like all the other victims.

Raising his head the next morning he felt much better even though he was still stiff from his ordeal. Sitting up he stoked the fire and added some wood and placed his hands over the flames to warm himself from the chill that was in the damp air. Reaching into the bag he took Tahou's breast that Angry Wolf had made into a tobacco pouch. He gently dropped it into the flames and watched as they turned into ashes. This was his last act to close out that chapter of his life. He chewed on a piece of jerky and decided he was well enough to move on, to get as far as possible away from the memories of the past few days. Getting up he strapped his backpack on and smothered the fire by throwing some dirt onto it. Picking up his rifle he started north out of the camp. As he passed the five dead Indians he bent down and cut his eagle feathers from Angry Wolf's hair. He stuffed them in his bag—he took back everything but Tahou's life from them. Facing north he left the area and never looked back again. Walking was difficult but it didn't matter, it would take time to heal the pain in his heart. He couldn't be certain the renegades might have friends, but he didn't think so. Alone with nothing but time on his hands again he had the vast empty wilderness to see what might lie just over the next mountain.

Wahnayah traveled north following the mountain range that would be known as the Rockies. Topping a mountain he stopped to catch his breath and rest his aching body. Clouds hung low just above the mountain and a light snow began to fall. Winter was near, it was already snowing up here in the higher elevations. The air was thin and that made it even more difficult for him. As he looked at the numerous snowcapped mountains in the distance he heard a lonely wolf cry. Then he moved on down toward the valley that spread out below. Several hours later the snow began to turn to a fine mist as he followed a creek that wound its way down off the top of the mountain. About halfway down he stopped and stooped down to cup some of the creek water. Walking onto a large rock that protruded out he studied the valley below. He could see no signs of life below. Just the lush green of the meadows and forest below; he should be at the bottom by dusk. The creek entered into a river that flowed across the valley making its way to the Pacific that lay far to the west.

As he had predicted, it was in the twilight of the late evening when he reached the valley. A clearing near where the creek entered the river would be a good place to make camp for the night. There was plenty of cover from the forest to hide his presence. A cold wind blew in puffs through the forest—a campfire would feel good to warm him. He gathered up enough firewood for the night and made a lean-to that he covered with tree branches and foliage. It afforded him some protection from the rain and should keep his wood dry enough. Soon he had a nice campfire burning bright, and he scooted back under the lean-to and wrapped the bear fur coat around his shoulders. He noticed he was getting low on jerky as he opened the bag. Perhaps he would stay in the valley for a while, do some fishing and hunting and rest his bruised body. He was far enough away from the dead renegades that he felt secure that no one was following him. A drop of icy water dripped from a limb and went down the back of his neck causing him to shiver. He chewed on the jerky and watched the flames dance as they consumed the wood. An owl hooted back in the forest, he figured it must be time for him to go on the hunt. He felt very alone—how he missed Tahou. It was quiet except for an occasional puff of wind that rattled the branches and the gurgling of the creek. Finishing the jerky he grabbed his rifle and laid it by his side then he lay back using his bag as a pillow.

Trying to stay dry during the night was difficult although the bearskin coat afforded him some protection. Visions filled his mind of the warm cabin and the soft warmth of Tahou's body against his. He yearned for her touch but he had to keep thoughts like that out of his mind. He must accept she was gone forever. Sleeping came in the form of dozing off then awakening suddenly only to doze again. Once during the night he sat up long enough to add some wood to the fire. He noticed the rain had turned into snow that slowly drifted through the trees coming to rest on the ground.

Awakening the next morning he glanced out from under the lean-to to see a light powder of snow covering the ground. His stomach growled. Hearing the sound of the creek made him think about how good some fresh fish would taste. Sitting up he took the bear coat from off his body and stretched. The soreness in his body reminded him of the renegades of a few days before. Touching the place on the side of his head he could feel it was scabbed over and healing because it itched. Wahnayah reached over and grabbed his bag and took the eagle feathers out and then tied them to the braids in his hair. He got up and found a long straight branch that he trimmed into a spear. With his rifle in his left hand and the spear in his right he made his way to where the creek joined the river. The snow crunched loudly under his feet as he walked across the ground. The rain had turned to sleet, then froze, then it snowed about two inches on top of that.

Walking as quietly as possible along the bank of the river he crouched down to look for any fish in the clear waters. Standing very still he saw from the corner of his eye a movement near a large rock protruding out of the water. Gently he laid his rifle on the ground at his feet. Then he raised the spear in the ready position watching the fish. It was swimming next to the rock. A quick thrust with the spear, the point penetrated the side of the large fish pinning him to the bottom. Reaching down under the fish, the point of the spear between his fingers, he lifted it up and backed up on the bank. Pulling his hand from under the fish he made a quick jerk of the spear and the fish hit the snow flopping. Jumping on the fish to hold it down he pulled the knife from the sheath on his side. He proceeded to gut and scale the fish. Then he bent down over the river and washed and cleaned the blood from his knife wiping it off on the snow. Picking up the rifle and fish he returned to the camp. He cut the trout into quarters and hung the meat over the fire to roast. He sat down and warmed himself eating some of the snow to quench his thirst. In time he checked the fish, it was well done. Cutting a large chunk from the fish he stuck the point of the knife in the meat and carefully ate some of it. The fish melted in his mouth it really tasted good for a change. Eating his fill, he would save the rest for later. He moved the fish that was left over to the side of the fire where it would be kept warm.

He checked to make sure the powder was dry in his pistol and rifle. Suddenly a movement down the river caught his eye. Quickly he grabbed his rifle and threw snow over the fire smothering it. Crawling on all fours he dropped down behind the trunk of a nearby tree. Pulling the hammer back quietly on his Hawkens he watched as the two Indians paddled past him then downstream. They looked to be in a hurry to him. He lay there behind the tree for what was probably an hour before he was satisfied they hadn't seen him or his campsite. He didn't think these two had any ties with the renegades, they were moving too fast and not looking for anyone. Clearing the snow from the fire he found some of the coals still smoldering. He sprinkled some kindling over the coals with his fingers and stooped down blowing on the fire. Soon it ignited and he added more fuel to the fire until it was back burning normal again. He picked up the fish and brushed the snow and dirt from it. Then returned it to the edge of the fire to keep it warm. Good thing he was far enough back from the river, he thought, or these two might have spotted him. He didn't want another incident like he and Kiska had with the Frenchmen. He would spend one more day here before moving on. Time was running out, he knew that, he would have to find a place soon to bed down for the winter. In the winter the daylight hours would be very short; he would have to build some kind of structure to winter in. Of course nothing as elaborate as the cabin he and Tahou had built.

As the day wore on into evening the snow began to fall much harder. He scooted farther back under the lean-to and wrapped up in the Indian blanket. The rest of the day he spent sharpening his knife, cleaning his rifle or pistol. Occasionally he would pull a piece of the meat from the fish and enjoy that while he could. He saw a rabbit back in the forest—that gave him an idea. Tahou had taught him how to construct a snare. He set it up about twenty yards back in the forest from his camp. Late that evening he went down to check it and to his delight he had a snowshoe rabbit in it. Grabbing the rabbit by the ears he hit the rabbit behind the ears with the back of his hand killing him instantly. Back at the camp he cleaned and skinned the rabbit and placed the carcass over the fire to roast. The skin he scraped, it would make some nice gloves to protect his hands from the cold. He could tell the wind was picking up as the tall trees swayed back and forth during heavy gusts. Once he had the rabbit skin scraped he made a frame to stretch it over and hung the frame on the back of the lean-to to dry. Glancing toward the fire he could tell the rabbit looked done. He pulled a hind leg off and ate the meat, it sure was a change. It was good that he came down off the mountain, the cold and snow was bad enough here in the valley. He could imagine how bad it must be up in the higher elevations. His stomach full of rabbit and trout he lay back under the lean-to resting his head on the bag. Pulling the blanket up over his body he belched the rabbit then he drifted off to sleep.

The next morning as he opened his eyes he could see that quite a bit of snow had fallen last night. As he looked down toward the river a puff of wind blew snow into his face, stinging his skin, and he threw his hand up to protect his eyes. Scooting out from under the lean-to he stood up and shook the snow from the blanket. He pulled the rabbit fur from the frame and put it into his bag—he would work on the gloves later. Blowing on his hands he could sure use them now but he wanted to move on and find a better place to bed down. The rapidly approaching winter was a warning that time was running out. He finished off what was left of the rabbit then covered the fire with snow. Next he rolled up his blanket and tied it to his backpack, shook his bearskin coat and slipped it back on. He was feeling better in the body every day—he was healing while the renegades were rotting.

Grabbing his rifle that was leaning against the lean-to he walked down to the river and looked up and down but could see nothing as far as the eye could see. He would follow the river upstream for a while staying well back into the forest for safety. Perhaps a tribe was camped along the river, and that was where the two in the canoe had come from. He definitely didn't want to run into anybody, he would go slow and be careful. He followed the river for a couple of hours then climbed a saddle between two mountains. He had no aspirations of fighting the cold and deeper snow in the higher elevations. As he topped the saddle he could see a few breaks in the sky. The sun was shining somewhere he could see the rays shining on the side of one of the mountains in the distance. The snow was still falling but very light now. A good day for traveling, he thought.

Several hours had passed since he left his last campsite. Making his way slowly around the mountain instead of trying to go up over the top he stopped to catch his breath. He looked down below and across to the next mountain but he could see nothing. Then his eye caught sight of a bald eagle in flight. Wahnayah watched as the eagle flew between the two mountains then he swooped down out of the sky in the far distance. There must be a large body of water over there somewhere, he thought. Those eagles were sure a sight to see—he kind of wished he could fly, must be something to be up that high. He remembered the eagles on the lake where he and Tahou had lived. They would swoop down and grab a fish half their size and then soar to their nest high in the trees. He marked the spot between the mountains where he had seen the eagle drop out of sight. That's where he would go.

As he followed around the mountain till he was between the two the terrain changed on him. The growth was a lot thicker and cedar underbrush made it very difficult walking. He would have to stop frequently to catch his breath, the air was much thinner than back in the valley. After several hours he finally made his way to the summit between the mountains. There was a plateau just ahead that was pretty clear of underbrush and only a spotty array of trees. He sat down on a large rock and glanced back over his shoulder from where he came. No wonder he had such a hard time pushing through the thick underbrush, the cedar concentration was heavy. The plateau ahead was perhaps a hundred yards or so across and about four inches of snow covered the ground. The walking would be much easier across the plateau. Picking himself up he moved on across the plateau, stopping at the far edge. It was late evening now. He sat down again. He was tired; coming through the thick underbrush had taken its toll on him. Looking into the vastness of the valley below he could see a small lake through the trees. That was where his eagle had been heading he was pretty sure. It was about a mile or so to the lake from where he stood. He would set up camp here—it offered a great vantage point, he could easily see anyone or anything—the plateau at his back, the ridge, then the vast valley below. A clearing just to his right would be where he could set up camp. He would drop off into the valley tomorrow and investigate the lake.

Wahnayah made his way to the clearing and set his backpack down. He scraped the snow away and gathered stones to encircle the fireplace. Next he picked up a handful of dead wood that lay near the camp area. He backed up and sat down leaning back against a large fir tree. He laid his rifle across his lap. The sun came out in the distance where the sky was clearing. A beautiful bright orange on the horizon that reflected also from the lake below—this was a breathtaking view to say the least. A movement off to the right caught his eye as he slowly turned his head. Cocking the hammer back on the Hawkens his eyes froze on the dark form coming up and walking along the ridge. A young deer, a yearling, pawed at the snow as it looked for morsels of hidden grass. The deer didn't even know that Wahnayah was but a few feet from him. Raising his rifle to his shoulder he took careful aim at the deer's neck. Squeezing the trigger the gun barked, smoke filled the air in front of Wahnayah, and the yearling collapsed dead where he stood. He could hear the echo of his shot recoil across the valley then back to him again. Dang, he would have to make himself another bow with some arrows. He never knew what happened to them, the renegades didn't have his bow and it was nowhere to be found in the cabin. The sound from his rifle could be heard for miles.

He sat quietly for several minutes; it was nearly dark by the time he got up and walked to the dark form lying dead. The young deer was not too heavy, and he threw him over his shoulder and walked back to where he would start a fire. He hung the deer from a branch on a tree by the neck. He started his fire and cleaned the deer from the light. He would cook some of the meat over the fire and the rest he would carry with him. Wahnayah's plans were to find a place to build a good enough structure to winter in. After skinning and cleaning the animal he cut a piece from the ham of the animal for dinner. The blood he cleaned from his knife and hands using snow he cupped in his hands. The skin he rolled up, he would use it after scraping it. The rest of the deer he cut into quarters; tying the legs together he would throw them over his shoulder and carry them with him tomorrow. He sat down at the fire warming his cold hands over the flames. It would be cold tonight, he could see a few stars shining through the thin clouds above. Taking out the Indian blanket he wrapped it around himself. Occasionally he would check the meat, turning it often until it was ready. Eating most of the meat he left some for breakfast in the morning. Lying down with his head next to the trunk of a tree he pulled the blanket over him. His pistol in his hand and his rifle next to his side he called it a day.

A small amount of snow fell from the branches of the tree he slept under hitting him in the head and awakening him. Startled he cocked the hammer on the pistol as he sat up. Realizing what had happened he let the hammer down and pushed the pistol into the scabbard on his side. Looking around the campsite the fire had just a fine bit of smoke rising from it. Stirring the coals he added enough wood to rekindle a small fire. He warmed the remainder of the meat from last night and ate it. Extinguishing the fire by covering it with snow he went about the task of gathering his things for the journey to the lake. He rolled his blanket and tied it to his backpack then slipped the backpack onto his back. The deer meat he threw over his left shoulder allowing the meat to dangle at his side. Picking up his rifle he started down the side of the mountain heading for the lake below. He walked slowly; about a foot of snow lay on the ground making the footing poor as he descended down. The added weight of the deer also made it difficult.

It took him several hours to descend to the valley floor; he had to stop occasionally to rest before moving on. Stopping once he ate the last of the jerky he had in his bag; he would make jerky from this young deer once he established his camp below. There was plenty of snow here in the valley and it was wetter than the snow up above. His feet and hands ached from the cold of the snow and dampness. Clouds had moved in again obscuring the mountaintop above him. At least the wind was not blowing as hard as it had been on the side of the mountain. He knew he needed some snowshoes; he would construct some as soon as he set up a permanent camp. After resting for a few minutes he pushed on toward the small lake. Within another hour he saw the lake through the trees—it was a beaver dam that created this body of water. They had dammed a place in the river. The forest was cleared around the lake from the beavers building the dam. This looked like a good place to winter because there was plenty of material to build a small cabin. Water was readily available and there was plenty of wood for fuel for his fire.

Clearing a large spot in the snow he dropped his backpack and laid his rifle on it. The deer meat he hung over a branch in a nearby tree. He took a 360-degree look in all directions. He was well hidden at the edge of the forest although not as perfect a place as he and Tahou's cabin, nonetheless efficient. He started a fire with some difficulty from the only wood available that was dry enough. No time to lose, he spent the rest of the day chopping logs and working on a shelter. This one he built in a square, he would leave a small hole in the roof where the smoke could filter through. Similar in fashion to the longhouses the Nootkas built. He worked up till it was nearly dark and the first day he had at least the walls started. As he bedded down the weather seemed to be breaking. He needed that—just a few good days, that's all he asked.

The next day he was up early. The sky had cleared—just what he needed. He first made some poles and cut and hung the venison up to dry. That done, he got back on working on the cabin. The sun came out and the snow began to melt away rapidly. He hesitated for a moment to rest and chuckled when he saw a family of beavers doing the same thing he was doing—working on their shelter. The hard work felt good, it kept his mind occupied and his wounds had healed nicely. A scar to the right side of his head was all that remained of the tomahawk chop. He felt pressed for time, he knew there was no way for him to know when the next storm would blow in. Sometimes a severe storm could blow in early without warning. He would also need enough time to stock enough jerky and wood to sustain him through the worst of the winter. The lake would be freezing over soon and fishing would become almost impossible to do. The shorter days would be so short as to eliminate much chance for a successful kill.

Cutting notches in the logs and using a lever he rolled them into place. His cabin began to take shape; it was more like a hut than a cabin. Wahnayah only took time out to check the meat drying on the poles and to eat. It would be large enough for him to store firewood in one end. By late in the evening of the third day he added the finishing touches to the roof. Walking around the building he was satisfied it would keep him warm during the hard winter ahead. He carried several large rocks inside, placing them in a circle around where he would keep a fire burning. The hole in the top he used the hide from the yearling to stretch over it. He could open and close it as needed during very bad weather. What daylight was left he spent chopping wood and carrying it into the cabin. As dark crept into the valley he lit up his fire and watched as the smoke rose then escaped through the hole in the roof. In the same way that Nootkas did he would keep this fire burning at all times. He covered the doorway with his Indian blanket, that should keep some of the cold night air out. Arranging the inside of the hut he was ready for bed early. Tomorrow he would be up early and spend the day hunting. Wahnayah cleaned a good place out on the floor next to the fire. Laying his rifle next to his side he curled up on the floor and used his coat to cover himself. Sleep came quickly after the full day.

The next morning he picked up his Hawkens and prepared to leave the hut. To his surprise a large bull elk was drinking water from the lake just fifty yards from the hut. Dropping down on one knee he used the side of the door hole to steady his aim. Taking a breath he let it out slowly then held it. Squeezing the trigger slowly holding the bead on the shoulder of the animal he felt the kick as the rifle barked. The elk fell to its knees then regained its footing. Wahnayah reloaded his rifle as quickly as he could while watching the elk. The animal shook his horns then turned to walk back into the forest but he staggered and fell forward into the ground. By then he had the Hawkens loaded, he sat there watching from the doorway for about half an hour. Satisfied the animal was dead he left the cabin and walked slowly toward the elk. Pulling the hammer back on the rifle as he neared he came in from the rear between the elk and the bank of the lake. The beautiful animal lay still; he kicked him in the butt hard. A bullet hole just behind the shoulder, a heart shot, he was dead all right.

Letting the hammer down he laid the rifle across the animal as he pulled out his knife. Then he opened the animal up from the bottom of the neck down to the groin. He reached in up to his elbows and pulled the insides out, he would save the heart to eat later. Throwing a rope up over a tree branch he tied one end to the elk's horns, the other end he wound around his waist and started backing up, pulling the animal halfway off the ground. The elk was high enough to skin. Then he rolled the hide up and carried it up to the hut. He would scrape it and prepare it later. Returning to the site of the kill he cut the carcass into quarters. After several trips to the hut he was ready to cut the elk into strips to make jerky from most of the animal. He cut a chunk from the ham—between that and the heart he would have enough to eat for several days. Checking the venison, he found it was just about ready—he would hang those inside the hut. The next four hours he spent cutting the elk and hanging the meat on the poles. This should hold him over for quite a while. In the evening he scraped down the hide and stretched it tight against the side wall. In a few days he would take the hide and beat it to soften it up—it would make a nice flap for the doorway. He would need the blanket and bear coat to keep warm when it got colder.

Under the light of the fire he cut another slice from the heart. He stuck his finger through the large hole from his bullet. That's why the animal hadn't gone far—he was amazed at the strength of the elk to regain his footing. The horns he hung next to the doorway of the hut. He remembered the rabbit fur in his bag. Walking over he reached in the bag and took out the soft warm fur. Sitting cross-legged on the floor he took his knife and made a pair of gloves that covered his palms. His fingers would be exposed but the extra covering for his hands would keep them warm. He sewed them up from strips of leather he cut from the deerskin. After working on them for a couple of hours he tried them on—they felt good. They would keep his hands warm in the cold months to come. Opening the flap on the door he looked out at the little lake in front of his hut. He could see the reflection of the partial moon just enough so that you could make out shadowy objects. Closing the flap he returned to the fire throwing a couple of large logs on—it wouldn't be long before he would turn in for the night. Curling up next to the fire he laid his rifle next to his side. Tomorrow he would try his luck at fishing—he had seen several trout swimming in the lake down by where he killed the elk.

The next morning he was up at the crack of dawn. He grabbed his rifle and spear and pulled the flap back and walked out into the dawn of a new day. He took a deep breath and then exhaled watching the smoke that blew out. It was a cool morning all right, and he stood there looking all around to see if he could see anything. A flock of seven ducks flew up from the lake, circled it once then landed on the far end of it. They wanted to distance themselves from this human that disrupted their feeding. Assured he was the only human in the vicinity he made his way to the bank. Wahnayah had made a sling for his rifle from leather straps he cut from the deer hide. Slipping his head through the sling he positioned the rifle at his back. The spear in his right hand he waded in the shallows of the lake looking for the dark form of a fish. He saw one just ahead, he took one step very slowly, set himself and threw the spear. It hit the water with a splash, and grabbing the back of the spear he held the fish down and reached under the fish then walked to the bank. He shook the fish loose far enough on the bank that it could not work its way back into the water. He repeated this strategy until he had three nice trout flopping on the bank.

Gathering the fish he ran a strap through their gills then he walked back to the hut. Outside he laid the fish down and slipped the rifle over his head and leaned it against the wall of the hut. Sitting down on a large log he grabbed the fish one at a time and scaled and gutted them. Peering up into the sky he noticed clouds moving in as the sun disappeared. Looked like another storm coming in. He would clean these fish and return to the lake for more. He gathered most of the elk meat and hung it inside the hut. Returning to the lake he speared five more fish—he would cook two and hang the rest in the hut. It was evening by the time he had finished. He checked the elk hide—it was just about ready, so he took it and beat it with a stick until it was soft. Then he unhooked the blanket from the front door and replaced it with the elk skin. That would work better as a door than the blanket. It would seal out the dampness better. He tried shutting and securing it and was satisfied it would stay shut in a heavy wind.

Just before dark a few flurries began to fall as the temperature dropped considerably. The wind began to blow. He glanced at the door flap—it moved in and out but seemed secure enough to hold. He sat on the floor moving the fish occasionally that roasted over the fire. The flames danced from the wind draft that blew in through the cracks in the walls. A few snowflakes caught his eye as they drifted down from the hole in the roof. He stood up and adjusted the flap to close the hole some. That would keep most of the snow out anyway, he thought. He wrapped the blanket around himself as the temperature dropped in the hut. Checking the fish, he found it was ready, and he reached over and pulled some of the hot meat from the stick that held it. Blowing on it he sat it on one of the stones that encircled the fire. When it was cool enough he picked it up and ate it. He thought about the berries that Tahou picked in the forest—they would be real good with the fish, he thought. He felt better now he had the hut, enough food, and wood stored to sustain him for maybe two or three weeks. It would be tough to make it in such a confined area but after what he'd come through he would make it. After consuming most of the fish he felt sleepy. He jumped when the door flap popped—the wind was picking up outside, looked like it was really blowing to him. Lying down close enough to feel the warmth from the fire he pulled the blanket up over him. He dozed off as he watched the shadows from the fire dance on the walls of the hut. Feeling for his pistol next to him he grabbed the grip and held it as he fell asleep.

A heavy puff of wind during the night awakened him when the flap came loose he jumped from his place and ran over to secure it again. It was very cold in the hut as he added several large logs to the fire. Crawling back under his blanket he tried to sleep but the storm raging outside kept him awake. Tahou was much better at stuffing the cracks on the cabin than he was. His body ached when he thought about her lying next to him on cold nights. Then all of a sudden a large pile of snow fell on him coming through the hole in the roof. Jumping to his feet he brushed the ice-cold stuff off of his body. Cursing to himself he reached up through the hole and attempted to clear the snow from the flap. This was a real blizzard blowing outside. Closing the flap and securing it tight he reached in the bag and put his rabbit clothes on. Damn, it was cold, but he was a lot further north than the Nootka village. He reached and grabbed his coat from the hook where it was hanging. He slipped his arms into the sleeves and pulled it up around him. Then he pulled his hands from the gloves and placed them over the fire trying to warm them. A chill came over him as he noticed snow seeping in under his door flap. Nothing he could do but ride out the storm for now. With the wood he gathered earlier he could make some snowshoes. With the amount of snow that had already fallen he would need them. He would sit there and try to stay warm and work on the shoes till daylight came. No use trying to sleep.

Morning came but the storm didn't let up. Wahnayah noticed the door flap was not popping back and forth. He felt the elk hide door, he could tell there was a large pile of snow behind it. The snowshoes finished he bent down and tried them on—they weren't perfect but they would have to do. He ate some more of the fish for breakfast. Later in the day it sounded to him like the wind had died down some. Grabbing his rifle he walked over and loosed the flap; a big pile of snow pushed through it onto the dirt floor. He would have to dig out the door, it was completely covered in snow. Putting his gloves on he began to dig a hole through the snow. Once he had to stop and warm his hands before he dug some more but eventually he saw daylight. Crawling through the hole to the outside world he couldn't believe it—a good four to five feet of snow had fallen and it was still snowing. A large drift reached all the way to the roof on the door side of the hut. The snow came down almost sideways as he glanced toward the little lake. It was nearly frozen over; winter was here in a hurry. It was apparent to him he couldn't stay here through the winter. Soon as there was a break he would take his chances and move west toward the Pacific. Digging what firewood he could from the side of the wall he carried it back into the hut. He pulled a large piece of bark from one of the logs and used it like a shovel to dig as much snow as he could away from the door. Finally he walked back into the hut and secured the flap behind him. Checking the jerky hanging from the roof he packed as much as he could that was ready. Soon as he hit the trail again he knew it would be a steady diet of jerky. He took down some of the fish and prepared it for roasting over the fire. Better enjoy the fish while he had it.

The storm lasted two more days and finally on the third day the winds subsided and the sky cleared enough for the sun to pop in and out of the clouds. This was his chance, he would head west. He rolled up the blanket and tied it to the top of his bag. After securing the snowshoes to his feet he picked up his rifle and left the hut. The air was frigid but it was clear as he started his journey. The snowshoes worked well, they kept his feet above the wet snow. He looked back at the tracks that led away from the hut. The mountains loomed in front of him; he would have to find a way to go between them. He didn't want to have to go over. All day he pushed on finding a way around the mountain. Stopping only occasionally to catch his breath. He covered his mouth with the bandana as the cold air burned his lungs.

For five days now he had pushed on in a desperate trek. During the night he would burrow in the snow to try and find some warmth. As he dropped off the other side of the mountain he was nearly frozen; he had to find someplace to warm up. Panic began to enter him as he realized he had to find a cave or a gully somewhere where he could start a large fire and warm his frozen body. He knew he was very close to frostbite if he didn't already have it. Suddenly his snowshoe caught on something buried under the snow, tripping him. He tumbled over and over down the mountain trying to catch something to stop him but to no avail. Then his head struck something that stunned him. He rolled on a few more feet before coming to an abrupt stop when he crashed into the trunk of a pine tree on the side of a frozen creek bed. The blow to the ribs took his breath away. He attempted to get up but his head was spinning so he sank back down then fell over unconscious. A small trickle of blood dotted the snow from the gash on the back of his head. As he lay still against the base of the tree it began to snow again, and as it slowly started covering his body he dreamed of Tahou and him swimming in the lake. Would this be the final chapter to Wahnayah's life? Would this very land that he had come to love so much claim him now?

Chapter 8

A Tlingit war party returning from an attack on a neighboring tribe, to teach them a lesson, followed a frozen creek that would lead them to their village. They were not normally a warring people, but they'd had enough, they must stop this stealing and encroachment on their land by the Haidas. Ankawoo, the leader of the war party, spotted something lying against a tree almost buried by the snow. Holding his hand up for the rest of the group to halt, he motioned for two of his men to investigate. Ankawoo at first thought that it was probably a dead animal. One of his men bent over and brushed the snow from the lifeless form. Then motioned to Ankawoo that it was not an animal but appeared to be a Chipewyan. Ankawoo joined them and helped as they uncovered the strange individual. Much to his surprise this Chipewyan was a white man with long fiery hair. Ankawoo took the Hawkens and instructed one of his men to strip him down to his buckskins. This party had staged a successful raid further up the coast. They had taken much spoil and slaves also. The village was in flames and disarray when they made their hasty retreat.

Wahnayah could hear voices as he fought to regain consciousness. The three men pulled him up roughly and tied his hands then slipped a noose over his neck. Wahnayah's head was still spinning as the group began to move again. After moving several hundred yards his mind had cleared enough for him to make out what was going on. As he recollected what had occurred to him he felt a pain on the side of his head. He remembered tumbling down the hill, then seeing the tree, then blackness. Reaching up with his tied hands he felt a large lump on the side of his head. The Indian closest to him slapped his hands back down. As he looked forward he could see seven individuals, all tied together with nooses around their necks. He did not recognize these Indians but that was not a surprise, he had traveled quite a way. A sick feeling welled up in the pit of his stomach. He knew his misfortune had left him in trouble once again. The fall hadn't killed him but what lay ahead might.

This group led by Ankawoo seemed to be interested in him, as he listened to them talking and pointing at him. They had not seen such a person with red hair before. The little contact with white men was from the long boats that they traded with. They were accustomed to seeing people with black hair and dark eyes. This strange individual was wearing clothes that Chipewyans wore. They were puzzled but they would have time to find out once they reached their village. Suddenly without warning Ankawoo motioned for the group to stop. They were pushed to the ground roughly by the braves. Ankawoo and seven of his men sat in a group and ate while four guarded the slaves. He told his men this one with the red hair and light eyes he had heard from the elders of such a people but he had never seen one till now. Soon the party were fed and they moved on; the slaves were given nothing to eat. They were almost at a trot as they moved quickly toward their village. If any fell they were hit across the back with leather straps. They didn't stop again until it was nearly dark when Ankawoo motioned for them to stop. His head throbbing Wahnayah fought to catch his breath. Bending over he cupped some of the snow in his hand and ate it. Suddenly there was a blow across the back from a whip but it was worth it. As the party sat down for the night to rest two slave women were released to serve them. All the slaves including Wahnayah huddled close in a circle trying to keep warm from the cold night.

They had been on the move for two days since the party had found him. As they dropped down off the side of a mountain he could see a river below through the tall trees. A light snow fell but the temperature was much warmer than back where he had come from. The party continued following the river for another three miles then he saw smoke rising through the trees. Several longhouses in a line sat back from the river close to where the tree line started. He could see three large totem poles standing approximately forty feet high in front of the buildings. One of Ankawoo's braves ran from behind the group toward the village hollering loudly. Wahnayah could hear the village break into a frenzy as they realized the party was returning. The noise seemed to get louder as they approached the center of the village. The slaves were forced to their knees near the front of the largest longhouse. The people screamed at them and hit them with sticks and stones as the slaves huddled together.

Wahnayah noticed one individual approach the group wearing a flat, very colorful hat with a blanket wrapped around his body. He figured this must be the chief or shaman of the village. Then the villagers circled the group as this individual came close. Ankawoo with head bowed approached and Wahnayah heard him call him Yakutat. They laid the spoils of their raid at the feet of Yakutat for him to inspect. He picked up some things and others he kicked at with his foot. Then he walked from one slave to the other inspecting them. He stopped when he got to Wahnayah, he bent over and felt his hair between his fingers. Motioning to Ankawoo he grabbed Wahnayah's noose and jerked him up. He towered above Yakutat as he stood up looking into his dark eyes. Wahnayah was struggling to breathe from the noose that was very tight around his neck. Yakutat touched the designs on his buckskins and murmured, "Chipewyan." Then Yakutat spoke in his native language pointing at Wahnayah as everyone went very quiet. Wahnayah could only guess but he figured his life wasn't worth much at this moment. It didn't matter much anyway. In a few minutes, he thought, he could see himself joined with Tahou again. Yakutat shoved him back down roughly to the ground. Wahnayah pulled the noose to loosen it so he could breathe. Then Yakutat spoke and the women were divided among several families in the group. Yakutat kept the majority of them for himself.

The only ones left now were the five males, including Wahnayah. Yakutat spoke and one of the squaws ran into the longhouse and returned sporting a large Spanish sword. She bowed low as she handed the sword to him. Then one of the male slaves was picked out from the group and dragged screaming to Yakutat, who stood waiting. The Haidas brave began to chant as he sat, legs folded under him on the ground. Then Yakutat stood behind him, raised the sword high above his head and with one swipe he severed the slave's head. The village broke into a pandemonium when Ankawoo took the lifeless head by the hair and stuck it on a pole. Yakutat handed the sword to the squaw, and she wiped the blade clean then took it back into the longhouse.

Wahnayah wondered what was to come next. The sword that Yakutat had—he wondered where he got it. Perhaps he traded for it or maybe he took it from a dead Spaniard. Ankawoo dropped the pole that had the head into a hole dug in the ground in the center of the village. Then Yakutat walked toward Wahnayah and he figured it was his turn to die. But the chief grabbed him by the noose and jerked it. As Wahnayah stared at the chief, Yakutat pulled him toward the largest of the structures that was in the very center of the longhouses. Inside the dwelling was similar to what he had seen in the Nootka village. The center of the building was the lowest point with a large fire burning circled with large stones. Around the walls of the building was a ledge built up about three feet from the floor. Yakutat grunted and pointed to a place near the doorway and shoved him toward it. He was puzzled why had the chief not finished him off like the other guy. The other males were passed out to other families, so perhaps they were the lucky ones, they would get to be slaves. Maybe he was saving the rest of them for another time—he could speculate all day but for now he was alive. He felt weak from his injuries and the many days without food. He tested his binds, but they were tight and he was unable to loosen them. Besides there were too many eyes watching his every move. Curious kids would come by and stare at him, then their mother would speak and they would quickly leave.

A Tlingit longhouse contained many family units that lived along the long wall that encircled the building. At the very back of the building was another room and this room was reserved for royalty. Yakutat and his family lived inside this room. Those people with position in the tribe would be closest to the chief. All the others sat around the outside of the wall and the most insignificant nearest the door. Here is where the slaves would be kept. The large fire that burned constantly in the center of the building must never go out. It was the women's responsibility to cook and keep this fire burning. The children's responsibility was to keep a steady supply of wood available. Around this fire is where the women would work and congregate and do their socializing. Even when the weather conditions were poor the children were expected to go out and get wood. Social standing inside of the tribe as well as between other Tlingit tribes nearby was of the utmost importance to them. There was no chance to escape, they had guards at the door.

He scanned the room looking at the many beautiful blankets and artifacts that were everywhere. The only openings to the building were the round doorway and a hole in the roof to allow some of the smoke from the fire to drift out. The hole above the fireplace had a door that could be closed in very severe weather. Even so the smoke hung low in the building causing one's eyes to water. Suddenly a squaw walked toward him with a rather large knife. She motioned for him to put his hands out. He didn't know whether to obey her or not. She might be getting ready to take a finger or hand off. Reluctantly he held his hands out and she reached between, cutting his binds. She turned and walked away without any further ado. He reached up and loosened the noose from around his neck, slipping it over his head. Coiling the noose he laid it next to his side. Reaching up with his right hand he felt the lump on the side of his head. He could tell it had receded some. He felt very hungry and thirsty but thought better of doing anything but sitting quiet. Considering what he had come through the last few days he was lucky to still be breathing. At least his head wasn't stuck on a pole out in front.

Ankawoo had a place along the wall next to Yakutat's room. He must be one of the big boys in the group, Wahnayah thought. Ankawoo had his knife hanging on his side. Everyone seemed to have forgotten he was among them. Thoughts of Tahou came into his mind. He could understand now how she must have felt as a slave. He didn't like the feeling. Studying every move they made he would learn their ways of doing things. Sometime if they didn't kill him he would get his chance to regain his freedom. Main thing for him to do now was just stay alive if possible.

An old squaw from Yakutat's quarters came toward him. She had a brightly colored basket in her left hand and a long limber stick in her right hand. He noticed the basket was filled with what looked like dried fish. Reaching into the basket she tossed him a small fish. Then she handed him a wooden bowl that was filled with water. He nodded his thanks but she showed no emotion as she walked away. Sipping some of the cool water from the bowl helped to revive his dehydrated state. Next he took a small bite of the dried fish. He could have eaten rocks he was so hungry but it wasn't too bad. This was a good sign, he thought, if they were going to feed him then he figured they wanted him alive.

A little later the old squaw returned. He handed her the bowl and tried to talk to her in sign language but she ignored him. Once while he sat there a little girl came by and reached a finger out and touched his arm. He smiled at her but her mother yelled at her and she quickly left. They'd talk to him sooner or later—the Chipewyan clothes he wore were confusing them. He sat there all evening and it was as if they had forgotten him altogether. He knew that was wishful thinking. They had kept him alive for some reason.

Night fell—he could see it was dark outside through the door. The Tlingits were settling down for the night. Two new guards came inside and stood at the doorway next to the slaves. No way for him to escape, he curled up and tried to stay warm. They had stripped him of his backpack, so there was nothing for him to wrap up in. He could only wonder what tomorrow would hold for him. One day at a time, he could only count his blessings—he was still alive, but for how long he couldn't know. He needed rest, he'd gotten almost none since they found him. Lying against the hard floor he dreamed of Tahou and Kiska, his friend—those were better times.

He awoke abruptly the next morning when he felt a sting across his back. As he quickly rose up sitting on the floor, he remembered his situation. The old squaw stood over him along with the other slaves. She was yelling at them and hitting them with a whip. He reached at the whip but one of the guards at the door hit him in the shoulder with the back of his spear. Then old woman pointed him toward a younger squaw standing behind her. Getting to his feet was difficult—he was stiff, his body was still very sore. Wahnayah towered over the old woman's squatty frame but she had the power and authority over him for now. The old woman motioned with her hand for Wahnayah to follow the young squaw.

He followed her out the door and one of the guards at the door came along behind them. The woman pointed to a pile of animal bones outside the door. She motioned for him to pick them up which he did reluctantly. Stooping down he started picking up the bones then he felt a blow to his shoulder as the guard hit him with his spear. He motioned for him to go faster. Once his arms were full of about all he could carry the woman told him to follow her. Just outside of the village was a place where they piled their waste. Wahnayah dumped the bones in the pile. They kept doing this over and over till there were no more bones. Then he had to help the children gather firewood and haul it back to the longhouse. The children taunted him throwing small stones at him as he toted the wood to the building. The slaves were used like pack animals to do all of the heavy work in the village. Somewhere around midday they stopped and all returned to the longhouse.

The old squaw kept yelling and taunting him and jerking on his braids from time to time. She was an ugly old wrinkled-up woman with half her teeth missing. Every time he got close to her, her breath nearly gagged him. She was important, she roomed with the chief back in the royalty room. He figured she probably was the chief's mother but he didn't know. Then she yanked him down by pulling on his hair. He sat back down in his place along the wall. Thinking and biding his time—she would get hers if he got half the chance.

Wahnayah watched as a young woman carrying a basket came toward him. He recognized her as one of the slaves that had been brought in, in the same group he was with. Quickly she bent down and placed a fish and some water at his feet, being careful not to make eye contact with him. He figured she couldn't be more than sixteen years old or so. The girl bowed her head when the old woman came near. He heard her call the old woman "Munaka." Munaka shoved the girl forward as if to hurry her up with her duties. As the girl hurried on her way Munaka slung the whip hitting the girl in the back. She grimaced with pain from the sting of the whip.

While he was eating and before he finished his meal several of the slave women came through the door carrying baskets full of salmon. Munaka swung the whip at him but he ducked. She motioned for him to follow her. Stooping down she cleaned one of the fish, showing him how to prepare them for drying. She handed him the knife and pointed at the large baskets of fish. He knew what she wanted. Thoughts of jamming the knife in her old gut crossed his mind but he'd wait when the odds were better in his favor. The rest of the day he cleaned basket after basket of fish. The slave girls would pick up the cleaned fish then take them to the poles to be hung. Every once in a while if he slowed down Munaka stung his back with the whip. Stinking like fish, his hands hurting and his back burning from Munaka's whip, she pointed him toward a large boulder. He tried to lift it but it was too heavy so he rolled it down to the river.

The young men were stacking up stones to create a weir on this end of the river. The Tlingits used weirs to build traps in the river. They could then herd the fish into the weirs, trapping them. One of the braves would enter the water and could then easily spear them. This was a very efficient way of catching large sums of fish, especially during the salmon runs. Straining with all the might he could muster he slowly rolled the rock into position. Then Munaka waved for him to follow her as they made their way back to the longhouse. The water in the river looked inviting, he wished he could jump in and wash this stinking fish off of him.

Back in the longhouse, it felt good to sit down and rest his body. He couldn't understand why these people kept fishing and hunting when they already had plenty stored away. What he didn't know was that the Tlingits had yearly potlatch festivals. Yakutat would be matching his wealth against other villages. His only reason for still being alive was that he would be a highly prized commodity at the next potlatch. Looking down at his hands he noticed the blisters had ruptured exposing raw tissue. Spitting on his hands he rubbed them softly together, it helped some to ease the pain. Munaka called the door guard Yaqui, then she pointed at Wahnayah mumbling. She then turned and joined the group of ladies around the fire. They were preparing the evening meal.

He listened as he heard Munaka call a woman from the group that had been preparing the food. She called her Tikal. She treated Tikal very rough, which told Wahnayah she was probably a slave. Tikal brought food to the other slaves, feeding Wahnayah last. As she handed out the food he noticed that she had a Chipewyan necklace around her neck. Coming near he whispered to her in Chipewyan but she ignored him. He noticed she was very nervous and avoided making eye contact with him. Then she set his food down on the floor at his feet. She glanced toward Munaka. Munaka was busy with the meal and the other women. Tikal whispered in Chipewyan to Wahnayah that she was a slave and must be careful. He did not recognize her as one of the slaves that was brought in with his group. Her eyes kept a close watch on Munaka as she explained she had been a slave with them for seven years. Tikal asked him, "Where did you learn the language of my people?" No doubt with red hair he was not Chipewyan but she was puzzled by his clothes. He explained to her that his woman taught him the Chipewyan language.

Munaka, missing Tikal, looked toward the slaves and noticed she was spending too much time with Wahnayah. As Munaka moved toward them Wahnayah rolled his eyes. Tikal caught the hint and quickly left to return to her chores. Munaka growled at her and swung the whip but Tikal was too fast as she ducked, avoiding its sting. Munaka approached Wahnayah mumbling loudly, she swung the whip at him but he blocked it with his arm. He thought to himself if the old nag had to hit someone it might as well be him. In anger she kicked over his water and handed his fish to the slave next to him. No food tonight, this would be his punishment. It didn't matter to him, it was worth being able to talk to someone. He had learned much from her in the short time they were able to speak. She told him that they were afraid of him because of his hair. They believed his hair was the color of fire from the sun. He would be highly valued at the potlatch. He told Tikal that he had a woman named Tahou. Wahnayah told her that she had also been a Chipewyan slave. He had much more he wanted to talk about but they had to stop when Munaka came.

The rest of the evening he sat quietly watching. He felt like he had found a friend in Tikal. She would be able to tell him much about these people. This potlatch festival, he didn't understand what this was but figured he would learn in time. He had learned that the Indians were superstitious about red hair from his father. *Well, at least I have one thing in my favor*, he thought. So far no chance for escape—they kept a very close watch on him and the other slaves. He would work to win their confidence, then when they least expected it he would make his move. Take one day at a time, that's all he could do. His body ached from the long day of hard work and his hands were in bad shape. He thought, *Once I'm free I'll follow the coastline, go south.* A pain in his stomach from no food—that damn Munaka, if he got the chance he would wrap that whip around Munaka's neck and choke her to death.

It was late—the people began to settle down for the night. A couple of the women were still sitting by the fire. The smoke hung heavy in the building. The fish smell was heavy on his body but he was too tired to care. Lying back he curled into a knot trying to find a position that would be comfortable. Shadows flickered in the building as he pretended he was back in his cabin with Tahou. They could not strip him of his dignity, he wouldn't let them.

The next morning he was suddenly awakened by the sound of people shouting and running in the longhouse. He sat up quickly trying to understand what was happening. The men ran toward the door with weapons in hand. The women grabbed up the little ones and hid them in Yakutat's room. He grabbed at Munaka but she hit him with her hand and pulled away. Tikal came close and he asked her, "What's happening?" She told him the village was under attack. Standing up he noticed the guards were gone from the doorway. He needed a weapon, this looked to be his chance to escape. They would be too preoccupied with protecting the village. Moving toward the door Munaka attempted to grab him but he doubled his fist and hit her in the face. She fell over backwards and lay still, stunned and surprised by his move. All the able-bodied men were outside.

Stopping outside the door he could see men fighting everywhere. This was a bloody battle, many lay wounded or dead on both sides. No one noticed him as he eased in behind the large totem pole. A Tlingit warrior lay dead next to the totem pole, and he reached down picking up the bow and arrows. A tomahawk whizzed past his head, sticking into the totem pole as he ducked. He was going to have to fight his way out of the village if he were going to escape. Looping the quiver over his head it rested on his back. Then he reached back and pulled one of the arrows from the quiver and loaded the bow. The Indian who threw the tomahawk came running straight for him. Pulling the string back on the bow he shot an arrow, hitting the man between the eyes. He screamed in pain and collapsed dead at his feet. Stooping down he took the knife from the dead Indian's hand and shoved it in his pants.

Reloading the bow quickly he glanced to see which way was best out of the village. A hundred yards to his left was the forest, this was the shortest path to freedom. As he fought his way toward the forest there was Yakutat on his back struggling to keep the Haidas warrior from planting his knife in his chest. Without thinking he shot an arrow at the warrior penetrating him through the neck. Only the feathers were visible as he tumbled off of Yakutat to the ground. Quickly Yakutat shoved the dead Haidas from him and struggled to his feet. Staring at Wahnayah a look of surprise was on his face to see that his slave had saved his life. As he turned toward the forest the Tlingits surrounded him. The battle had been won and the Haidases retreated back into the forest. Their weapons trained on him he dropped the bow and knife to the ground. Damn, if only he hadn't stopped to save Yakutat he could have been free. His eyes staring into the warriors it was evident that his attempt to escape was futile. His hands and feet were tied to the totem pole. He could only watch as the women of the village slowly came out to tend to the wounded. There was weeping as many held or touched their dead that were scattered about. It was a sad day for the village as many men had been lost to the battle. Why had he saved the chief's life? He couldn't answer that question. In any case he would be watched even closer than before.

Munaka came out of the longhouse rubbing the red spot on her face from his fist. Picking up a stone she threw it at him hitting him in the stomach. He doubled over fighting to catch his breath. She picked up another stone but Yakutat grabbed her hand and yelled at her. Looking angrily at Yakutat she slowly let the stone slip from her fingers, dropping to the ground. Struggling to catch his breath a grin came over his face. At least he received some satisfaction from knocking her on her butt. She would make him pay in the future but it was worth it. The battle had been a hard-fought one but the Tlingits had repelled the invaders in the end. Then Yakutat motioned for Wahnayah to be untied. He would join Ankawoo and the others as they carried the dead to the burial room. The Tlingits constructed a special building that was set aside for the dead.

Late in the day he was returned to the longhouse. He noticed a change in how he was being treated. At mealtime he was given an extra portion of food to eat. Munaka even spared the whip across his back. He was given a blanket to cover himself at night. There was much grieving in the village—several of the men had lost their lives in the battle. Yakutat placed guards around the village just in case the Haidases decided to come back. They had taken many loses themselves—he doubted they would be back. As he lay back his mind went through the events of the day. He had come very close to being free again.

The next morning Yakutat sent Ankawoo and a small party of braves to make sure that the Haidases was gone from their territory. Wahnayah would spend the day helping to remove the dead enemy bodies from the village. About a mile from the village was a cave in the side of the mountain where they took the bodies. A period of grieving was in order—the dead were cremated and placed in the burial building. Slowly things began to get back to normal. He figured his new status made him somewhere between a slave and a true member of the tribe. If he had it to do over again he'd let Yakutat move on to the happy hunting grounds while he made his escape.

A week had passed when Ankawoo and the party returned. Wahnayah noticed as soon as they entered the village something was wrong. Ankawoo was sick along with the others in the group. Wahnayah recognized it right off, they had the measles. He had heard stories of simple diseases like this wiping out complete tribes. Yelling loudly he ran to meet them holding his hands in the air. Yakutat became angry and confused with his action. Using sign language he asked them all to stop where they were and asked for Tikal to interpret. Yakutat waved for Tikal, who came between the two groups. Wahnayah told them that they were sick and that he knew about this sickness. He told them that he had this same disease as a child. He warned all the rest of the village to stay away and asked Yakutat if he could have the building where the women went to have their children. Ankawoo and the six others who went with him followed Wahnayah to the quarantine area. Munaka instructed the women to place blankets outside the building. He asked Munaka to keep plenty of cool water available from the river. Inside those who did not yet have the disease were instructed to keep the room dark. Wahnayah sat down next to Ankawoo and asked him what happened on their journey. Ankawoo said they came upon a village where many had died from the sickness. They became frightened and left but on their way back to the Tlingit village some in the group, including Ankawoo, began to feel bad. Wahnayah knew that the illness usually took about seven days or so to run its time. He only hoped that he had caught these men before they infected the entire village.

That evening Ankawoo and two others became very ill with high fever. He stayed near the men all night applying cool compresses to their heads. He elevated their heads slightly as this helped some. The room was kept warm with the only light coming from the fire. He wrapped his bandana around Ankawoo's head and over his eyes. Why he felt compelled to help these people, he couldn't answer that. After all he was still a slave. Ankawoo shook from the fever but the only thing Wahnayah could do was try and keep him cool.

By the fourth day Wahnayah was doing his best to stay awake. The entire group was sick with the measles now. Munaka sent Tikal to bring water and food on a regular basis. She would set it down outside of the building. She told him that the village was very concerned about this sickness. He assured her that he was doing what he could but that he was concerned about two of the men. She told him that the others had cremated the dead and the village was back to normal other than what was going on with them. He told her to convey to Yakutat that they would have to replace this building, for safety they should burn this building. Returning to the cabin he noticed that Ta Kaa (Sleeping Man) did not appear to be breathing. Checking his pulse, he was right, he had lost this man. Taking his blanket he rolled him up in it. Walking back to the door he motioned for Tikal, who came to the cabin. He told her they would need to prepare a place to cremate Ta Kaa, that he was dead. Later that evening he lit the fire and burned the remains of the dead Indian. He had to be very careful to keep any of the others from contracting the disease.

By the seventh day Ankawoo's fever had broken and he was beginning to show signs of recovery. Ankawoo was strong enough to help with the others and give Wahnayah time to rest. Kooshkan succumbed to the illness later that day. The rest of the group looked like they would make it. As they did with Ta Kaa, they rolled Kooshkan in his blanket and burned his remains in the evening. They would stay in the hut for another five days before he was satisfied that they were all well enough to join the others.

After twelve days in the hut all signs of the measles were gone. All of them left the hut and he burned it to the ground. They all stood watching it burn. Then they all went to the river and washed their clothes and bathed before rejoining the tribe. Yakutat was well pleased with him for saving the entire village. Even though he was still considered to be a slave he was given more freedom than the other slaves. He was allowed to speak with Tikal without worrying about Munaka's whip. They would be having a potlatch soon, she told him. His chances for escape were getting better.

Chapter 9

The village returned to normal. There attention was transformed back to preparing for the upcoming potlatch. Wahnayah had never heard of a potlatch and he really had no idea what to expect. He figured it was just more work for the slaves. The event was probably the most important event that happened to the Tlingit people all year. The many Native American tribes in the Northwest enjoyed a rich environment of lush forest, abundant fishing with many streams and the Pacific Ocean nearby. The forest was teeming with animal life. So unlike the Indians in the desert West and Plains there was no struggle for resources to sustain them. Tikal told him that Yakutat would be competing with the other Tlingit chiefs for wealth and high standing. Yakutat had held this honor of being number one for many potlatches. Yakutat owned many slaves, many children, and great supplies of food, furs and artifacts. A large fleet of canoes that were built so well that they could be taken into the open sea. The Tlingits would even hunt whales on an occasion. The seals were used for their oil and fur, plus they collected much food from the sea. Yakutat's reputation was well known among the Tlingits that were spread along the Northwest. The entire village worked hard to replace what had been destroyed in the battle.

A Tlingit village would be broken down into groups called moieties and a individual could identify himself or herself as either Raven (Yeil) or Eagle (Chaak). Members of one moiety would refer to the other side as "the opposite side." Marriage was formerly allowed only between persons from opposite moieties. Within each moiety would be broken down even further into smaller units called clans. A clan would govern the social, ceremonial, and political life of the Tlingits and linked them to their ancestors and future generations. Names of children in the clan would be obtained from a deceased member, thus continuing the rebirth of an individual. The house or longhouse was a subunit of the clan and was occupied by several closely related families. Within the longhouse were a leader, his brothers, their wives and children, and the house leader's matrilineal nephews. Wealthy chiefs could hold as many as twenty to thirty slaves. Slaves were usually captured in war or purchased from southern tribes and did all the tedious and hard labor. Yakutat was from the Eagle moiety. This great honor and position had been preserved in his clan by his father, which passed it down to him. His wealth and status power were the strongest among the Tlingits.

They were just two days away from the potlatch festival. The village was in frenzy as they prepared for the very important event. Yakutat sent Tikal to take a message to his favorite slave. The message would convey to him that during the potlatch ceremony, to show his power and great wealth, he would free Wahnayah as a slave. He would not only be freed but he would become part of their clan. Because Wahnayah had saved his life in battle this would be his gift to Wahnayah, his freedom. It would be done during the potlatch to honor both men. Tikal told him her story that she had been traded to Yakutat from one of the southern tribes. She had been a slave since she was about ten years old. She said the Tlingits were curious to know where this white man dressed like a Chipewyan had come from. Wahnayah then began to tell his story of his traveling from very far away. He told her about another slave girl that became his woman, then of the pursuit of the renegades who destroyed his home. The near-death situation when they captured him, then how he escaped. How he had fallen down the mountain knocking himself out, how Ankawoo and the war party found him nearly frozen. Then she stopped him and told him she was sent to bring him to the council meeting—they must be going now. Both left together as they made their way to the chief's chambers.

As they entered the room through the doorway he recognized all the important members of the village. The smoke hung thick in the room, so much so that his eyes stung and watered. Yakutat sat at the head of the group. On his head was a beautifully decorated hat made from cedar bark. Around him was wrapped a chilkat robe with designs of his clan in vivid colors. They called the chilkat robe naxein. Yakutat motioned for them to sit down next to him on the left side. Normally females were not allowed at these formal meetings, but because Tikal was interpreting for Yakutat, he would allow it. Tikal was instructed to squat behind Wahnayah and whisper between he and Yakutat. Then Yakutat raised his hand and the room became quiet. Yakutat spoke in his native tongue and Tikal spoke in Chipewyan to Wahnayah. "I, Yakutat, greatest of Tlingit chiefs, will give Wahnayah his freedom during the potlatch. This slave saved my life from sure death during the battle. Not only that, but he saved the village from certain destruction from the dreaded disease of spots. Only two were lost when the whole village could have been destroyed. This will take place during the potlatch." Then he turned and faced Wahnayah as Tikal interpreted. "I have one condition—your freedom but you must become one of my warriors."

Wahnayah hesitated then nodded his head. He knew he didn't really have a choice—to turn down Yakutat would be an insult. Then Yakutat turned back toward the circle of men and said, "Whomever disagrees let him speak now or from now on be silent of this matter." The room was quiet. Yakutat had a beautifully carved and decorated pipe that he passed around the group. Wahnayah was not allowed to join in as a slave. They all took a puff then passed it to the next individual. Then Yakutat told Tikal that he and Wahnayah must leave the room and return to their duties.

As they entered the main part of the longhouse Tikal was met by Munaka. Wahnayah continued on, joining the men as they brought fish in to be cleaned. Tikal explained to Munaka what occurred during the council meeting. As Wahnayah prepared the great baskets of fish

Ankawoo joined him. Ankawoo handed Wahnayah his knife, the one that Kiska made for him and that they had taken from him. Wahnayah nodded his head and took the knife and strapped it on his side. Pulling the knife from the sheath he continued cleaning the fish. This had been a good day. Ankawoo, once his captor, now had become his good friend.

Finally the day of the potlatch was upon them. The village increased in size dramatically as other Tlingit tribes joined them in the festivities. Yakutat was very generous, which was a big part of showing his wealth. Dancing was everywhere as this was an important part of their religion and culture. The sound of drums could be heard throughout the village. The men tested their skills in competition. Ankawoo gave Wahnayah a bow and a quiver full of arrows. Wahnayah was allowed to join in the archery competition. His friend Kiska had taught him to become very good with the bow. All the Tlingits were impressed with his ability to hit the target and to load and shoot the bow rapidly. Ankawoo smiled in approval of his newfound friend and soon-to-be warrior.

As evening began and all congregated around the fire the people came to see which of the chiefs would be found to rank the highest. Yakutat, dressed in his finest hat and chilkat, gave away many great gifts as they traded wealth. The final competition would be between Yakutat and Xoots to see who would be the greatest. Yakutat motioned for Wahnayah to join him. Then he announced to the people that he was giving this, his greatest slave, freedom to become one of them. A hush came over the crowd as all eyes turned on Xoots. All of his twenty slaves he did not have a slave to match this one. It was plain for all to see that Yakutat would remain at the top. Xoots regretfully bowed out of the competition. Then all returned to their festivities of eating and dancing, thanking the Great Spirit for their much abundance. The shaman joined the dancing as they prayed to the spirit for a prosperous year to come.

The potlatch lasted for four days, then the visiting people began to slowly return to their homes. Wahnayah was directed to his new place along the wall. He would be next to Nokatu and Puya, the newest of the married couples in the village. No longer a slave, he would take his place fishing with the men at the traps. Large numbers of fish would be caught during the salmon runs. One day Ankawoo took Wahnayah and two others and they canoed down the river to the sea. They hunted seals, which were sunning on the rocks near the shoreline. They would approach very quietly and when close enough they shot them with arrows or speared them. The seal's fur was highly sought after because it resisted water and was very warm. They used the oil for softening the leather and weatherproofing it. Wahnayah killed three large seals. He was also impressed with the ease with which the large canoe slipped through the waters. Very little effort was needed with the oars. They moved in and around the small islands searching for seal and halibut. With a boat full of meat they headed back to the village, entering the mouth of the river. The rowing against the rapid-moving waters proved to be difficult as the men strained hard on the oars.

The canoe slipped up onto the bank as many individuals, including the slaves, ran to unload the fish into baskets to be cleaned. Ankawoo and the group split up, returning to the longhouse to eat and rest after their long trip. Later they would make another trip to the Great Salt Lake to hunt the great fish. The small hunting group had spotted several whales feeding along the shoreline. Several days would pass before this trip would be attempted.

Yakutat gave the order for four boats and sixteen braves to man the largest of the canoes. The men loaded the canoes with the large harpoon spears that would be used to kill the whales. They left late, they would camp along the river and enter the sea at daybreak. That night along the river they planned their strategy. Two boats would position the whale between them. The other two canoes would follow as backups, coming alongside to assist or to take over pursuit should one of the lead canoes run into problems. They were up early and entered the sea just as good light covered the land. Yupik, an old man in the village who came along primarily for his wisdom, taught Wahnayah to throw the harpoon. Ankawoo would man the harpoon in the left lead canoe and Wahnayah in the right canoe.

They slowly moved out into the open waters in search of the great fish. Then Yupik yelled, "Yaay, yaay!" as he pointed to a large gray whale as all spotted the great tail rise and then disappear. All dug into the canoes hard as they moved forward in hopes of being close enough when he surfaced to spear the great fish. Yupik pointed right as they maneuvered further right. The old man was wise, as the great fish surfaced and blew water high into the air. The men canoed with all their strength, then Ankawoo lifted the barbed spear high and threw it. Almost simultaneously Wahnayah did the same from the right canoe. Blood covered the clear water as both harpoons dug into the whale. The rope smoked as it quickly uncoiled from the front of the canoe. The long rope hit the end then with a jolt that jerked everyone's head back the canoe jumped forward leaving a wake as the canoe cut through the water.

Hanging onto the bow to keep from being tossed from the canoe, Wahnayah picked up another harpoon. Then slack came into the ropes as the whale headed for the surface. Quickly they pulled the rope into the boat and carefully coiled it. Ankawoo and Wahnayah readied for the next attack on the great fish. Just ahead they could see as he came to the surface then blew water clear. Steadying himself Wahnayah threw the heavy harpoon into the side of the whale. A pink blood covered the water—he had pierced a lung. The whale rolled on his side. Yupik waved for the other two canoes to join them as the great whale blew out his last breath filled with blood. They moved forward and connected ropes to the front of the fish and they slowly pulled the whale toward the mouth of the river. Ankawoo raised his hands to the sky as they all gave thanks to the Great Spirit for this great catch. Every muscle strained as they oared hard against the massive weight of the large beast.

After several hours they reached the mouth of the river, and throwing lines on the bank they tied the whale securely. All sat catching their breath and resting, then Ankawoo jumped onto the whale and with a very large knife began to carve great hunks of meat from the whale. They filled the canoes as full of meat as they could carry. Yupik would return to the village and send back more canoes to collect the great fish. Ankawoo and Wahnayah would remain with the whale. Ankawoo and Wahnayah watched as the canoes disappeared up the river. The two men collapsed to the ground from exhaustion—it had been a very difficult day. Ankawoo indicated they would be back by morning; he would take the first watch and Wahnayah should rest. Ankawoo didn't have to tell him twice as he laid his head against his bag.

The next morning a large contingent of canoes filled the river as they began to quickly cut the whale up. To Wahnayah they looked like a large group of ants. By noon there only remained a pile of large bones as the canoes moved upriver toward the village. What a feast that night as the village rested and gave thanks to the Great Spirit, who had blessed them greatly.

A light snow began to fall as the tribe labored to finish their preparations for the first signs of winter. The daylight hours were much shorter now and darkness would come early. The women gathered near the fire to socialize and weave baskets. The men gathered in the council chambers where Yakutat had summoned them. Tikal joined the men to interpret for Wahnayah. Wahnayah had picked up some of the Tlingit language, but he still required the help of Tikal. Yakutat raised his arm high and all went quiet in the room as he began to speak. He turned his attention toward Wahnayah. Yakutat said, "You were once my slave. My eyes saw you less than a human being. But I have watched you in battle and how you have become one of us. You are a great warrior and hunter. You have brought great honor to the Tlingits." Wahnayah listened as Tikal whispered the words of Yakutat in his ears. Yakutat continued, "Because you have chosen to become a Tlingit I wish to honor you with a gift. You shall have the pick of any of the unmarried women of the village. Only my daughter is forbidden to you."

Wahnayah swallowed and showed no other emotion as he thought to himself. He had not thought of ever having another woman in his life outside of Tahou. To reject the chief's offer was a downright insult. The only woman he could think of was Tikal, so he spoke to her in Chipewyan and asked her if she would be his woman. Tikal sat with a shocked look on her face and slowly nodded her head yes. Then Wahnayah spoke, "You were once my enemy, Yakutat, but we have become friends and you are my chief. I am not worthy of such a great gift but I thank you and I choose Tikal."

Yakutat stared into his eyes then nodded and said, "So it shall be done." Then Tikal was ordered to leave the council as Yakutat passed the pipe around the room. Each man puffed the pipe then swept the sacred smoke across his head.

Later, before dark as he prepared for sleep, his thoughts were on his emotions toward being attached to another woman. He did not feel the same warmth toward Tikal as he did toward Tahou. She was not as beautiful as Tahou but she did have some of the same traits and she spoke Chipewyan, which he knew well. If he wanted to continue to live he must go through with this wedding. Yakutat had told him the wedding would take place in three days. Because both individuals were slaves of Yakutat's at one time he would supply the gifts to make the wedding official. Tikal would win her freedom by being married to Wahnayah since he was now considered a member of the tribe. The Tlingit wedding would be enjoyed by everyone except for the lucky couple. They would sit together in the center of the room while the rest of the village feasted and celebrated their union.

The next morning Tikal was allowed to move in with Wahnayah. In Tlingit customs the couple were allowed to set up housekeeping prior to the marriage. Wahnayah decided to stay out of her way and let her arrange things the way she wanted them. He joined the men fishing in the river. Although fishing was not as good with winter approaching, still it was an excuse for him to get out of the way. The women sat giggling and pointing at Tikal as she busily arranged their place. She felt so honored that this strong warrior had chosen her to be his wife. She would love him and be a good wife; she knew he once had another love but she would make him forget her. Wahnayah's respect among the men warmed her all over, no longer a slave but now the wife of a great warrior. She knew better than Wahnayah just how rare it was for a Tlingit slave to win their freedom. Surely the Great Spirit had heard her cry for freedom.

As night fell and Wahnayah returned she met him with a large portion of food. He did not speak to her but sat staring into the fire as he ate his meal. She felt sad because he did not pay much attention to her, but they needed to get to know each other better. Finishing the meal Tikal slipped under the covers of their bed. She gently removed her clothes and laid them beside the bed. Wahnayah felt so guilty to even think of making love to another woman besides Tahou. Tahou's memory burned in his mind as he glanced toward Tikal and where she lay asleep.

He knew she was waiting for him but he just couldn't bring himself to join her. Tahou's playful silly way had charmed him so much. Tikal was an older, more mature woman about twenty-eight years old. Others were watching him, he knew he had to join Tikal. She tried to understand why he did not want to come to bed. It was late when he slowly crawled back to where Tikal was waiting in bed. Undressing down to his pants he slipped under the covers next to Tikal. He rolled up against her back but could not touch her. Gently she took his hand and placed it over her bare breast. He cringed; it had been a long time since he had been that close to a woman. She felt him move and she knew it would take him time, she would be patient and in time she would gently coax him. He would come to love her. They both slowly fell asleep. His steady warm breath against the back of her neck made her feel secure and wanted for the first time in her life. In his mind he pretended that he and Tahou were once again in each other's arms.

Tikal was up early the next morning and joined the women congregated near the fire who were fixing the morning meal. The rest of the tribal women treated her as though she had always been a part of their group. To shun her or treat her as a slave could bring punishment to them; after all she was one of them now. She returned to Wahnayah and handed him his breakfast. Tikal looked at him but he avoided eye contact with her. She gently touched his muscular shoulder with her hand then returned to the group. The talk in the village was of the upcoming wedding. It would be a big event as all weddings were. Tikal watched as Wahnayah left the building and joined the other men at the river. All day he struggled with his emotions; he would be giving up Tahou for good if he gave in to Tikal. Ankawoo and the other men figured his quietness was because of his soon-to-be wedding. It was a big step in a man's life when he took on a woman and family in the future. Little did any of them realize his real struggle.

The cold winter wind blew across the village tucked in the valley. It would be their wedding day and still he had not taken her. Tikal was sure tonight would be the night—this was their wedding day. The village was a bustle of activity preparing for the celebration and wedding. The women dressed Tikal in her best buckskins with beautifully designed artwork, they combed her long black hair and decorated it with feathers of many colors. Wahnayah spent the morning in the smoke house preparing himself. The Tlingit belief was that the smoke brought spirits that would prosper and strengthen their union. Then he went to the river where he bathed. Returning to the village he dressed in his best buckskins, a pair of beautifully made moccasins was given to him by Yakutat's wife. Munaka braided his long red hair and tied an eagle feather in his hair. A second feather she tied to his wrist to represent the devotion that the two of them would have to the Tlingits.

The time had come. Wahnayah and Tikal were brought to the center of the longhouse near the fire. Furs were placed on the floor for them to sit on. Squatting down and crossing their legs they sat side by side with their backs to the fire. Yakutat motioned for the ceremony to begin. The festival began as they sat quietly watching as several of the villagers danced around them. Dancing was a big part of the Tlingit custom. The dances would tell stories or coax the spirits to prosper this couple with many healthy children and long life together. The couple sat motionless till it was very late in the evening when Yakutat came and tied their wrists together. This signified that they were now married. Then the village crowded around as they were ushered out of the longhouse to a small hut just at the outskirts of the village. They would spend several days in this hut together before they would be allowed to return to their place. The villagers sang and danced as they followed the couple to the hut. Tikal opened the door, and clasped together they entered the hut. Wahnayah shut the door to the delight of the village as they shouted then returned to the festivities to leave the couple alone. Even though he wasn't exactly ready for a wife tonight was the beginning of a new chapter in his life.

They entered the hut; a fire was burning in the center of the room. There were berries and fresh fish cooking as Wahnayah reached over and untied the leather strap around their wrists. Tikal touched his hand gently but he did not respond. They sat down and ate the meal that had been prepared for them. After finishing their meal Tikal undressed and stood in the dim firelight in front of Wahnayah. He made no advance toward her. She crawled under the fur cover of their bed and waited for him to join her. Wahnayah, eating some of the fish, stared into the fire. His mind could only picture Tahou. Several hours passed before he joined Tikal, who had already fallen asleep waiting on him. He slipped under the cover and laid his arm over her waist. Tikal waited for his advance toward her but it never came as the two fell asleep.

The next morning Wahnayah was up early. He opened the door and went out and sat outside the hut. Ankawoo and some of the men at the weirs looked at each other and grinned as they stared at Wahnayah for a moment. Ankawoo laughed as he told Gaax Kaa, "He must need some rest from his new wife." Gaax Kaa laughed as they returned to their fishing.

Wahnayah glanced toward the totem poles and could see some activity, he could see the guards high above that watched over the village. He sat down brushing away the light snow next to a tree. Leaning back against the tree he could see a golden sky shone over the valley as a new day dawned on the horizon. Tikal opened the door and beckoned him to join her for breakfast. Ankawoo snickered under his breath as he watched Wahnayah enter the hut. He joined Tikal at the fire, but he avoided eye contact with her—she must be wondering what's wrong with him. She handed him food to eat and he sat staring into the fire. She moved close to him. Tikal then spoke and told him she understood about Tahou. She said, "Tahou is gone, she will not be coming back. Your journey through life continues. She would not want you to grieve for her." She put her arms around his neck and hugged him putting her cheek against his. Then she placed his hand on her breast and gently bit at his neck. Slowly he began to respond to her touch. As they made love he couldn't completely erase Tahou's memory from his mind; he remembered their days at the lake.

The couple returned to their place as the honeymoon came to an end. Much giggling and talking went on at the fire as the others surrounded Tikal. Wahnayah left the longhouse and joined the men at the weirs. Ankawoo chose a group of men to accompany him on a hunt. Some of the young boys would be coming along to learn how to hunt. The band consisted of Ankawoo, Wahnayah and four others that were broken down into bands of three men. Wahnayah took one group and

Ankawoo would take the other group. Ankawoo pointed to Wahnayah to go north; he and his group would go south, and they would meet back at this point before dark. Wahnayah motioned for his group to follow as they moved slowly north going into the forest. A light breeze was blowing in his face as he followed tracks made by a deer. They moved slowly, taking a few steps then stopping, being careful to crack no twig or make any quick moves.

As they approached a small creek Wahnayah raised his hand for the others to stop. Slowly bending down he scooped up some of the mud from the creek bank and rubbed it over his face. The others followed his example then standing up he motioned for them to continue the hunt. They moved deeper into the forest. Occasionally he would stop to point at the tracks on the trail or a broken twig.

Suddenly Wahnayah dropped to his knees, and with bow and arrow ready he froze. The others did likewise watching him intently. Upon his knees he cocked the bow and gently let the arrow slip from his fingers. The arrow swooshed through the forest, hitting the large elk in the neck. He shook his head trying to remove the arrow then Xoots, standing behind Wahnayah, fired his arrow. The arrow hit the animal in the shoulder causing him to momentarily collapse to his knees. Then Yaqui fired his arrow hitting the animal at the base of the neck. By that time Wahnayah was ready and fired another arrow hitting the elk just under the ear. It groaned and collapsed to the ground, rolled over on its side and went still. Wahnayah motioned for them to squat down and watch the animal for several minutes. When they were assured he was dead they slowly approached the creature with bows drawn. Wahnayah kicked the elk in the rump but it showed no signs of life. They dropped to their knees and thanked the Great Spirit for this beautiful and powerful animal.

Wahnayah pulled his knife from the sheath on his side and stuck the point into the animal just behind the ear. Yaqui and Xoots rolled the animal over on its back then Yaqui began to gut the animal. Pulling the heart out he took a bite and passed it around to the other two. After Yaqui finished skinning the pelt from the animal he rolled it up and tied it. Xoots constructed a travois and they loaded half the animal onto it.

Wahnayah and Yaqui took the other two quarters and the three men slowly headed back to the rendezvous point. It took them most of the rest of the day to reach the river. Sitting down next to the river each took turns drinking some of the water then sat down to rest. Soon Ankawoo and his group joined them. Ankawoo's group had only killed a small deer and was pleasantly surprised at the success of Wahnayah's group. Yaqui, Xoots, Naagasei, and Xaat each carried a quarter of the elk as they returned to the village. Ankawoo and Wahnayah would carry the deer and the elk skin. The group moved quickly hoping to reach the village before dark.

The band reached the village just at dusk, and the villagers excitedly ran to see what the hunters had killed. Yaqui and Xoots both agreed that Wahnayah's arrow killed the elk and that he should get the pelt. Wahnayah took the rolled-up pelt and gave it to Tikal—it would keep them warm on cold days. The weary hunters made their way to the fire in the longhouse. Tikal brought Wahnayah a double portion of food to eat. He patted her on the butt as she returned to the fire, and looking back at him she gave him a smile. Yakutat was well pleased with the hunt; they would go again tomorrow before the winter worsened.

Later that evening Wahnayah was asked to tell his story of the elk hunt. As he spoke and Tikal interpreted for him all listened intently. They all laughed at his animated way of telling stories and how the elk laughed at them. He said the great elk thought that there was no way these three could bring him down, but they fooled the great beast. The elk laughed within himself over their small arrows but when they cut deep into his body he realized he had made a mistake. When the story telling was over Yakutat and the men joined him in the council room. Passing the pipe around he blessed the hunt and thanked the Great Spirit for his generous gift. They would hunt again tomorrow, but for tonight they would all celebrate with dancing and drum music Tikal felt so proud of her husband—he had been the one to make the kill. He was such a strong warrior and a great provider for his family and the village. Tikal enjoyed the festivities but Wahnayah went to bed early—they would be on the trail for another hunt tomorrow, and he knew he needed to rest. His body ached as he crawled under the covers—it had been a long day. He hoped tomorrow would bring the same success they had enjoyed today.

Sometime during the night Tikal joined him. She brought warm water from the fire that she rubbed on his sore back and legs. She could not replace Tahou. She wouldn't even try, but she could love him and help him to forget. Wahnayah was glad that he had married Tikal. She was a good woman and he did not desire to travel down the journey of life alone. Tikal was right and he knew it. Tahou wouldn't want him to be unhappy, she would want him to go on with his life, as he would have been toward Tahou if the situation were reversed. Tikal would make a good mother—she was a hard worker but yet very softhearted toward those she loved. Lying down next to him Tikal snuggled up close to him locking her arms in his. His hard strong muscles made her feel very safe as they fell asleep. Life had been good to both of them and now they were free in each other's arms.

Chapter 10

Two years had passed since Wahnayah and Tikal had become husband and wife. Peace and harmony had blessed the Tlingit tribe with prosperity and great wealth for their chief, Yakutat. Tikal had ached to give Wahnayah a son but so far she had been unable to get pregnant. Wahnayah was now in his middle thirties. As Wahnayah sat on the riverbank, his feet soaking up the cool waters, he watched as an eagle drifted toward the snowcapped mountains in the distance. His mind wandered back to his old friend Kiska and he wondered how he and his people were doing. So many stories could be told since the day he waved good-bye to the Nootka village as he set out on his journey. He felt assured within himself that he had made the right decision to venture to this part of the world. Yes, he had known love, fear, sadness and pain, and he had weathered it all and managed to become a much wiser man than then.

As the time went by a line of low-hanging clouds darkened the sky and then a few flakes of snow slowly drifted to the ground. He watched them for a few moments then the wind picked up as a chill filled the air. His thoughts went back to Keewatin and how concerned he was the first time he knew he was not alone in his little valley. Tahou—what a beautiful woman she was—he still missed her but Tikal had filled that empty void deep in his heart. He felt warm air on the back of his neck and for a moment wondered where it could be coming from. Then Tikal put her arms around his neck and bent over whispering in his ear. What she told him made him quickly stand up and jump high into the air. The villagers turned, looking at him strangely and wondering what had happened to their friend. She was pregnant with their first child. When he had just about given up, a great miracle had blessed them. He hugged Tikal, lifting her feet off the ground, he kissed her on the ear and laughed like a small child. He told her how happy he was to hear such good news. The child should be born in late summer some time. Then she told him, "I must return to my work now." Wahnayah watched her as she walked away until she was out of sight entering the longhouse. Tikal had been true to her word—she had found her way into this man's heart and now she would repay him with a son. He joined the men fishing in the river. Soon it would be cold and much time would be spent inside.

As the days passed Tikal slowly began to show signs of the life that grew inside of her. Wahnayah became almost a pest as he did everything he could to help her. This winter turned out to be one of the hardest anyone could remember in years. He worried about Tikal after two of the small children in the village took ill and died. Nothing the shaman could do nor Munaka's great wealth of experience with herbs could keep them from passing into the next life. Wahnayah felt very badly for the young parents who lost the children; it was so hard to watch such young life end so soon. As they sat eating the dried elk meat and berries Tikal suddenly groaned when the baby jumped. Wahnayah, concerned, asked her, "What's wrong?"

She took his hand and placed it on her abdomen and he felt as the baby kicked again. They both laughed when Tikal told him, "He wants to come out and play with his father."

The weather broke some, so the men headed down to the river. Some fished, some made up small hunting bands. Wahnayah followed those who ventured down to the river—he didn't want to be too far if Tikal should need him. Most of the river was frozen over other than a small stream where the waters moved swiftly. The air was bitterly cold but all desired fresh meat and they would do their best to spear some fish. The men worked hard catching the small sum of fish they were able to spear. Between the fish and the hunting group who brought back a couple of deer everyone would get a chance to have some fresh meat. The adolescent girls and boys took the fish and cleaned them for the women, who manned the cooking. The day was very short so they had very little time for gathering much of anything. The smaller children accompanied by an adult female went into the forest and gathered wood for the fireplace. It was good to leave the longhouse if even for a little while.

Back in the building Wahnayah warmed his hands over the blazing fire. He took off his moccasins and handed them to Tikal to place near the fire for drying. The aroma of the fresh-killed game cooking over the fire filled the longhouse. Wahnayah stood at the door for a moment watching the snowfall. He noticed the guards high on the mountains that encircled the village. The Tlingits had to keep guards against attack from enemy tribes. They sent out bands to raid other tribes themselves from time to time. Tonight he would stand watch himself; it was a bitter cold night and he wasn't looking forward to it.

Tikal handed him his evening meal and sat down beside him. Wahnayah would relieve Yaqui on the northern peak. The village was strategically set in the valley surrounded by hills with the creek spilling into the river only a few hundred yards below. Upon attack there was ample time for the guard to send an arrow below to warn of intruders. Wahnayah patted Tikal on the stomach; she was beginning to show the child that grew inside. Not long from now she would have to leave him and move to a hut that was set aside for birthing children. She would be considered unclean until after the child was born. They both listened to the strong winds that blew. Tikal told him she would pack him some extra food to keep him warm. He would take his Hawkens with him tonight.

Wahnayah sat finishing up his meal; he reached down and pulled the elk-skin cover over his shoulders. He watched as Tikal helped the women prepare the meal for the rest of the village. The children played and romped around the building pulling tricks on each other as all children do. Tikal brought food and began packing it into his bag; soon he would be leaving for his night on the northern peak. As she worked packing his bag he slipped his arms around her waist and gave her a hug. She smiled at him as she finished packing the bag. Picking up the bag he slipped the sling over his shoulder then grabbed his rifle, and bending over he kissed her on the forehead. She helped him put on his bear-skin coat then touched her hand and turned, walking to the door. As he opened the door snow blew into his face stinging his cheeks, and he quickly squinted his eyes. Bending over he slipped outside shutting the door behind him. He stood for a moment to let his eyes adjust to the darkness. He could see about three inches of snow covered the ground as he began to make his way up the trail toward the lookout point. He would be about two thousand feet above the village as he worked his way up. Soon he could see Yaqui leaning back against a large tree just twenty feet from him. He waved and Yaqui returned his wave as he struggled to his feet. The two men locked an arm then Yaqui picked up his belongings and headed down the trail to the village. Wahnayah cleaned away a place at the base of the tree. He laid a seal skin down to sit on; it would keep him dry from the wet snow. Looking down the trail he saw the last sight of Yaqui as he disappeared into the darkness. Wahnayah leaned his rifle against the tree and sat down on the skin. He made himself- comfortable, then grabbing the rifle he laid it across his lap. Looking below he could just see signs of the village and the light from the longhouse when Yaqui opened it to enter. Looking north he could see the large valley below, then another mountain in the far distance. He pulled the bear coat up tight around his neck as the wind whistled across the mountaintop.

Several hours passed since he relieved Yaqui. He remembered the extra food Tikal prepared. Leaning over he grabbed the bag, and opening it he took some of the jerky and bit off some and slowly chewed on it. He noticed the sky was clearing to the northwest—looked like the storm was passing. With the stars shining on the snow cover he could see much better down below. The chill in the air he could feel Tikal's warm body against his down in the longhouse. It would be good when his watch was over. He didn't like the idea of Tikal moving into the birthing hut but he would honor the Tlingits' custom.

The sound of a wolf hollering in the distance echoed across the mountains. They were probably on the hunt. It was very early morning now, the night slowly passed by. Occasionally he would stand up in the shadows of the tree to warm himself by moving some. Suddenly his eyes caught sight of something moving about two hundred yards below. There wasn't enough light for him to be able to determine if it were man or beast. Glancing back toward the village he saw all was quiet. He slipped his hands from under his bear coat and grabbed his bow and arrow. It would be quieter than the rifle and he didn't want to alarm the village if it were just an animal. He watched as the figure slowly moved up the mountain to within fifty yards of his location. Straining his eyes he saw that it was standing on two legs—it was either a man or a bear, he couldn't tell. It was too slender for a bear, it had to be a human. No need to be alarmed yet, there was only the single individual.

Keeping himself hidden behind the tree he now could see that it was a Haida. The Haida wore a mask that darkened his face. Then from the corner of his face he spotted other individuals coming up the mountain behind him. Reaching into the quiver he took out the arrow that was wrapped with oil. Striking the flint rocks together he lit the arrow. Drawing the arrow back he shot it in the darkness down toward the village below. The Haidas spotted him as the group moved rapidly up the mountain toward him now. Loading his bow he heard the whistle of an arrow as it stuck in the tree just next to his head. Drawing his bow back he let it fly. His aim was true as a Haida screamed when his arrow struck him in the chest. The Indian collapsed and tumbled backwards. The arrows buzzed as he grabbed his rifle and started moving down the trail to the village. He stopped behind a tree and reloaded his bow, and as he stepped back around he was hit with an arrow in the shoulder. Fighting against the pain he fired back hitting the man in the head. They were overwhelming him as he grabbed his rifle and started down the trail. A sharp pain in his side as another arrow pierced his left side but he kept moving, then another one hit his hip. He struggled and fell to his knees. As a Haida came at him he fired his rifle, dropping the man. Then a tomahawk hit him across the back of his head and he fell face down into the snow unconscious.

The guard at the door spotted the flaming arrow and opening it he yelled they were under attack. Ankawoo motioned for the men to get their weapons and to follow him. They formed a band and moved quickly in the direction of the flaming arrow. As they moved up the mountain they met the Haidas in hand-to-hand combat. Ankawoo saw Wahnayah lying on the ground just above with a Haida warrior standing over him. Pulling his bow back quickly he shot an arrow at the Haida who had his tomahawk ready to finish off Wahnayah. The arrow stuck the Haida through the neck as he tumbled backward dropping his tomahawk. Then the battle increased as more men from the village joined in the attack. The Haidas were outnumbered and their surprise attack had been foiled. Badly outgunned and outnumbered, they broke out in a run retreating from the Tlingits. The snow turned red from the blood, as many lay dead from the fierce battle.

Ankawoo ran to where Wahnayah lay in a pool of his own blood in the snow. He bent down and put his ear to Wahnayah's bloody mouth; he could feel a faint breath against his cheek. Wahnayah was alive but not by much. He yelled for others to help him as they picked up Wahnayah and carried him down the hill to the longhouse. Yelling as they came near the door Munaka swung the door open and directed them where to lay him. Tikal screamed in agony at the bloody sight of Wahnayah. They laid him on a mat near the fire. Munaka screamed out orders as the women went into action preparing to attend to his wounds. Squatting down beside Wahnayah she could only shake her head at the sight of him. It would take all she knew plus a miracle from the Great Spirit to save this warrior. Tikal stood looking over her man with tears streaming from her face. Munaka yelled at her to shut up, that she would do what she could to save her man. "I will not let your child be without a father," she said. The old woman had many years of experience dealing with herbs and potions. The shaman came and began to dance about praying and sprinkling his magic over the bodies of those that were wounded. Munaka gently cut away the clothes from Wahnayah's body. She surveyed the damage and then began to cut the arrows from his body. The old woman worked feverishly as sweat dripped from her forehead. She yelled and screamed at the other women and slaves, telling them what to do. Ankawoo and the other braves waited outside the doorway for word of how his friend was doing.

Many hours passed and yet Wahnayah hung on to life, much to the surprise of all. The old woman, soaked in blood and sweat, a weary look in her eye, worked on to save him. Standing up she sat down by the fire and looked into Tikal's eyes and said, "I've done all I can. It is between him and the Great Spirit now." Tikal grabbed Munaka's hand and squeezed it. "He is strong, Tikal." The shaman came close, blowing on a flute as Tikal bent down holding Wahnayah's hand. Yakutat put his hand on Tikal's shoulder; he saved the village.

Wahnayah's life passed through his mind as he lay in a delirious state. He saw his mother and father again. Tahou beckoned him to follow her but he fought, he still had things he must do. His dreams turned to nightmares as he hung upside down, a renegade slowly cutting away his skin. A faint voice caught his attention calling him in the distance; he struggled to clear his eyes and mind to see who it was. He drifted into darkness then again he regained his consciousness and slowly his eyes begin to clear. He focused on a shadow standing near him as his senses began to return. A slow *tap tap* of a drum, the beautiful sound of a flute playing a slow serene song, he remembered the battle. Wahnayah wondered if he was dead and this was the Great Spirit world. Slowly his eyes cleared and he could see it was Tikal rubbing his sweaty forehead with a damp cloth. The sound of the flute came from a woman who played as the shaman danced and chanted. Then he felt the pain from his many wounds as he groaned looking at the roof in the longhouse. Tikal began to shout that he was awake. He tried to sit up but Tikal gently pushed him back down. Tikal bent over him and gently whispered in his ear, "You are badly injured from the battle, Wahnayah. Rest now and regain your strength." She grasped his hand and it all came back to him. How did he survive? The last thing he remembered was being hit by a tomahawk. His head began to spin as he drifted out then to sleep. Munaka assured Ankawoo and the others that Wahnayah had passed his worst, he would recover in time.

Many days passed as Munaka and Tikal nursed him slowly back to health. Tikal feeding him told him he had lost much blood. Ankawoo helped Tikal as they helped him sit up. His head spun but slowly cleared as he sat there. As he looked over his body, only then did he realize how badly he had been wounded. He felt a sharp pain in his hip where the arrow had buried to the bone. Tikal handed him a bowl of stew mixed with herbs to help him with the pain. He slowly ate the warm liquid as his appetite began to return to him again.

Ankawoo sat down next to him as Tikal returned to her chores. "Wahnayah, my friend," he said, "when I found you a Haida warrior was getting ready to finish you off. My arrow found his neck." He hesitated for a moment then he continued, "My brother, it is good that the Great Spirit sent you back to us. You saved our village. There were many Haida lying dead near you." Wahnayah listened as Ankawoo finished his story. "Your bravery has saved our village; we are all very grateful to you."

Then Wahnayah weakly spoke, "I am no hero, Ankawoo. If not for your arrow, my friend, I would no longer be among the living."

Ankawoo and Wahnayah locked their arms together in a sign of brotherly love. Then Ankawoo stood up and said, "You heal, my brother, I must join the others. Soon we will hunt together again."

Tikal joined him and took his empty bowl. "You must rest, my husband, if you expect to have enough strength to hold your son," she said.

As he lay there quietly many from the village would come by and smile and give him words of encouragement. They were a truly warm people; he had made the right choice to stay and not escape. He had found his place in the world. It had been a very long and hard journey. Feeling pain and weakness he knew he must rest as he closed his eyes.

The cold winter began to give way to spring as the flowers began to bloom and the snows turned to rain. Wahnayah was getting stronger every day, and with the help of a crutch he was able to hobble out and watch as the men fished. He sat in the warm sun—it gave healing to his wounds. Tikal was very large with child as she wobbled around the village. Wahnayah poked fun at her from time to time but both were anxious to see their child. He tried shooting his bow but his fingers were still numb from the wound in his shoulder. Working his hand and exercising it was helping. Every day he was getting stronger and couldn't wait to be back to normal. Grabbing a spear he entered the river as the others watched him. Hobbling slowly along he jabbed the spear into a large salmon, and reaching down with some bit of pain he was able to drag the fish to the bank. Looking up he noticed as the men had stopped to watch him and when he dropped the fish on the bank, Ankawoo nodded his approval. His friend had come a long way back from near death to the point that he could spear a fish. Wahnayah pointed at the traps and said, "Oot xaat," which meant salmon in the fish traps. Ankawoo chuckled, as did the others, then they turned their attention back to the work at hand. Wahnayah had learned some of the Tlingit language and no longer needed Tikal to interpret for him. He thought about how Munaka, that crusty old woman, had performed miracles on him, as he slipped back into the river and speared another fish.

The village was in a state of anxiety as the word came to Wahnayah that Yakutat, the aging chief, had suddenly taken ill. Munaka and the shaman had been summoned to his side. Wahnayah thought if anyone could nurse him back to health it had to be Munaka and her bag of tricks. This time, however, it looked bad as the chief hung dangerously close to death. Koani, his oldest son, took over at the council meetings until his father should recover. Wahnayah remembered another time when the chief was a strong warrior and wielded the sword that he just knew would take his head off. But with time he too had come to love this old chief. In the council room was a solemn group, as they knew soon Koani would take over as chief. Munaka had run out of magic, it was just a matter of time till Yakutat joined those in the Spirit world. It was a bad time for this Tlingit village.

The tough old chief lingered for another week before he finally gave up. He fooled all of them and proved what a fighter he was even until death. Preparations were being made for Yakutat's funeral and the crowning of the new chief, Koani. First, however, there would be the mourning period, which was customary by the Tlingits. The Tlingits believed in reincarnation, that Yakutat would return through one of the newly born. The Grizzly clan would have the responsibility for the burial of Yakutat. Yakutat was dressed in his royal clothing and wrapped in his favorite naxein. A naxein was a beautifully decorated robe that was used to wrap the dead in. Wahnayah colored his face in the Tlingit tradition of sorrow for they had lost a great leader. Wahnayah cut a braid from his hair and placed it next to Yakutat's body so that he would remember him. The women cut their hair or singed it; all had their faces colored black for the eight days of mourning that would follow. The Grizzly clan prepared a great funeral to honor Yakutat because he was well respected throughout all the Tlingit tribes. Koani called for all to congregate at the center of the village to witness Yakutat's final journey. There was much wailing and mourning that stopped when the cedars were lit under his body. As the fire blazed Wahnayah wondered what the future of the village would be under Koani. The odor from the sweet-smelling cedar filled the village as the smoke rose high then blew south. They all watched until the fire had completely consumed Yakutat. Yakutat's cremated remains were gathered and placed into a beautifully designed wooden box and set in the burial building. Everything was quiet that evening as the end of one era had come and the beginning of another would start tomorrow. It was a time of uncertainty for all.

The next morning the village turned its attention to the ceremony for Koani. Koani dressed in his extravagant clothes, his hat made from cedar bark and wool woven together and colored in the bright Tlingit pattern. Yakutat's ceremonial cane was passed to Koani as a gift from his dying father that would be used during special ceremonies. Would Koani be able to match his father's honor during the famed potlatch ceremonies? Only time would tell as a day of festivities rang out throughout the village. Visitors from other Tlingit tribes came to join in as the villagers danced and sang to the new beginning.

A month had passed now since Koani had become the new chief. The village relaxed back into their everyday routine. Koani was proving to be just as ambitious as his father had been. Wahnayah knew that Koani was a brave warrior, he had seen him in action during skirmishes with their enemy, the Haidas. Wahnayah figured the village would survive nicely under the new chief's rule. Koani was a strong good-looking young man that knew his role well—after all, he'd had a good example to follow.

The time was late summer now and Tikal's time for delivery could be any day now. She had moved out and was staying in the birthing hut, as was the Tlingit tradition. It was hard for Wahnayah without his woman near his side. At the door of the longhouse he watched as the golden sun peered above the mountains to the east. Grabbing his spear he would spend his day at the river fishing. Ankawoo and a group had gone hunting in the forest but he decided to stay close to the village.

Down at the river the water was cool to his body as he sat down on the bank and dangled his feet. He still was stiff from his wounds but the pain had all but disappeared. Then someone touched him on the shoulder and he turned to see Yewatu's young daughter. Excitedly she explained that Tikal had gone into labor and that the child would be coming soon. Anxiety filled him of the thought that soon he would be a father. Standing up he entered the waters near the weir. He would keep himself busy, the suspense was killing him. He spotted a large salmon that he ran his spear through. One of the slaves waited for him to bring the fish and put it in the basket. He continued walking and spearing until the basket was full, then he climbed from the waters and sat down to rest his sore hip. The time seemed to creep by as he awaited the news. He worried that something had gone wrong as the hours clicked by.

Then late in the evening close to sundown Kageet came running to tell him the good news. Tikal had delivered a son. Wahnayah had to sit down—he couldn't believe it, he was now a father. Ankawoo and the others slapped him on the back congratulating him. Kageet waved for him to follow her. They made their way to the edge of the village where the hut was located. Munaka met him at the door and handed the little bundle to him. He was so light Wahnayah couldn't believe this was a little human being. Looking at his son he was so small and so fragile looking. Bending his head over he kissed the baby on the head then handed it carefully back to Munaka. The whole village could hear him as he let out a yell. Life always brought jubilation to the tribe as the drums and flutes could be heard playing throughout the village.

As is customary among the Tlingit women eight days must pass for purification before they can rejoin the tribe. Wahnayah couldn't wait to be reunited with his wife and new son. But finally the day came for Tikal to join him in the longhouse. The village was bustling with excitement as Wahnayah and his new family were brought back together. The couple decided to name the child, Gijook, which means Yellow Hawk.

In the longhouse Wahnayah took the child from the t'ook (papoose) and held him high for all to see. Many wondered if this child was Yakutat come back reincarnated.

The excitement over the new child quieted when word came that Koani was holding a council meeting. Wahnayah gently set the child back into the t'ook and handed it to Tikal as he followed the men to the council chambers. He entered the heavily smoke-filled room and found his place in the circle. Koani was already sitting at the head of the group in his ceremonial dress. Soon the room filled up as members filed into the room and took their places. The door was shut as the room was filled with murmuring. No one could figure out what the meeting might be about. Koani held his hand up and the room silenced as they waited for his words. Then he began, "My father was a great chief and I above all miss his presence. I ask that the Great Spirit give me the wisdom to lead and be a great chief as he was."

Then Koani indicated he would appoint his officers. He began to speak, "I choose Ankawoo, my trusted friend, to lead our tribe in times of battle. If Ankawoo should be killed or die then Wahnayah will be his second in command." Everyone grunted and nodded their approval at the chief's choices.

Then Ankawoo asked to speak and the chief nodded for him to go ahead. "I would have given my life for your father and my chief, Yakutat. I pledge the same honor to you, Koani. We grew up together and learned to fight side by side." Ankawoo finished talking and sat down.

Then Wahnayah stood up. "I pledge my life to you, Chief. Twice since I became a Tlingit the Great Spirit has given my life back to me. Yakutat handed me my freedom and recognized me as a Tlingit. I am Tlingit and will die Tlingit." All murmured with excitement at his words. Wahnayah sat back down.

Then Koani congratulated Wahnayah on a fine new son as he lit the sacred pipe. After taking two puffs he then passed the pipe to Ankawoo, who then passed it to Wahnayah and around the circle of men that attended the meeting. In turn each scooped the sacred smoke over his head. It was apparent that the same strengths that governed the tribe would remain intact. When the pipe had circled the room Koani dismissed the council meeting. Ankawoo and Wahnayah proceeded to the sweathouse, where they spent several hours praying and thanking the Great Spirit for blessing them and their village. Wahnayah then spent some time in his favorite place in the creek swimming and bathing before he joined Tikal.

These were good years for the Tlingit tribe. Little did they know that their world was on the verge of being turned upside down. The gold rush in the California area plus the constant flow of immigrants coming west would soon even reach the Tlingits. Word had come through the Tlingit tribes scattered along the Pacific coast that several ships had been spotted. Some had come to hunt for the rich seal furs and others traded with the Indians. The cold winds blew down from up north and they headed into another winter season. Wahnayah and Tikal were busy raising the new son, Gijook. But still in the back of his mind Wahnayah knew that eventually the white man would come. Maybe he just ignored it or maybe he thought they would leave this part alone. It was colder up here than along what would come to be Washington and British Columbia in the future. Occasionally Wahnayah would travel down to the Russian trading post in Nome and trade furs for powder and shot for his Hawkens. He preferred to avoid the white man altogether—there were always plenty of questions concerning his dress. Most of them were used to an occasional mountain man but this white man was definitely not in that group.

Tikal was sure a good mother, all right. The boy was doing fine—the only thing he didn't particularly like was the uncle did the teaching of the son. The Tlingit tradition gave this authority to an uncle, and in this case Ankawoo would do the teaching as soon as the boy was of age. He was well respected by Wahnayah but he wanted that duty for himself, nonetheless he would have to abide by the rules.

Wahnayah had the job of working with Ankawoo's son, Ax Yect. Ax Yect was about eight years old now and would accompany Wahnayah on hunting trips. He taught the boy how to read signs of the animals, their tracks and dung. They had become good friends and the young boy called him Nayah for short. They spent many hours in the forest and Wahnayah had him stand in the frigid water of the river for several hours to discipline him. It would be part of the boy's training to be strong and not cringe in the face of difficult and very uncomfortable tasks. Wahnayah was very proud of the boy, he exhibited those same strong traits that had elevated his father to his status in the tribe. He enjoyed working with Ax Yect but wished that it could be his own son.

One day he called, "Ax Yect, come get your bow, let's go into the forest." He let the boy go first as they walked one behind the other down the animal trail. If Ax Yect made any noise he would gently boot him with his moccasin in the rump. They walked very slowly and quietly then they moved off the trail a few feet as they started down an incline. Just below Wahnayah spotted a doe as she lay asleep in the warm afternoon sun. Ax Yect did not see her yet but Wahnayah very quietly touched him on the shoulder and pointed at the sleeping deer no more than twenty feet in front partially hidden by the undergrowth. Ax Yect quietly pulled the drawstring on his bow and Wahnayah did the same on his. The arrow swooshed through the air as the doe raised her head just in time for the arrow to pierce her neck. Startled, she tried to get up but Ax Yect was all ready to shoot and fired his second arrow hitting the doe in the shoulder. She kicked violently but could not regain her legs.

Wahnayah pushed on his shoulder to squat down as both sat watching as the deer's kicks became less violent and finally stopped. Wahnayah patted the young boy on the head, as this was his first kill. After several minutes, Wahnayah motioned for them to go to the deer. Quietly, with bow and arrow ready, they approached the deer and Wahnayah motioned to come in from the back rear side of the deer. Standing next to the deer he motioned for Ax Yect to look at the deer's eyes; they were a dark green color. Then both offered thanks to the Great Spirit for this kill. Wahnayah leaned over and whispered, "When the deer's eyes have turned this color he is dead." Pulling his knife from the scabbard he handed it to Ax Yect and told him to put his bow against a nearby tree. The boy rolled the deer over on its back and sat on its stomach. Wahnayah showed him how to clean the deer. He smiled at the facial expression the boy made as he pulled the bloody entrails from the animal. Wahnayah took the knife and cut the heart out and took a bite, handing it to the boy, who did likewise. Then Wahnayah patted him on the head as he instructed him to tie the feet together. Ax Yect wiped Wahnayah's knife on the grass and handed it to him. Wahnayah reached down and slipped the feet of the deer over his head as he picked it up and they headed for the village. Ax Yect grabbed his bow and led the way.

As the two returned to the village Wahnayah called for Ankawoo to come and told him that Ax Yect had made his first kill. This would be a big event in the village, as well as a step in this young man's life. All enjoyed a great feast as the young man was honored with an eagle feather for his hair. This was a sign that he had taken another giant step toward manhood. All listened as Ax Yect told his story with demonstrations of how the deer died when his arrow struck its mark. It was a great time of laughter and honor for the young man. As Wahnayah watched the festivities holding his own son he felt a closeness to these people that he had come to love. These were his people, he was a Tlingit. The party proceeded well into the late evening as the village feasted on the deer that Ax Yect had killed. He would get the skin but he would also be taught to share with the rest of the people. His mother would make a nice pair of buckskins that would depict the story of how this young boy, her son, stepped forward on his journey of life. As Wahnayah touched his son on the hand Ankawoo patted him on the shoulder at his approval, Wahnayah nodded. Both men had sons who would one day take their place as leaders of the tribe. Tikal came and took the baby as she told Wahnayah they had a big day ahead and they must get some rest. She rubbed his shoulder where the scar was all that remained of the battle. The cold outside caused his body to ache; he was no longer the young strong bull he once was. His journey through life had been a very long one, he was like an eagle wondering what might lie over the next mountain.

Chapter 11

It had been a year now since Koani had taken over for his deceased father, Yakutat. The young chief had learned much from his father, and there was no doubt in Wahnayah's mind that in time he would be identical. Although their first potlatch had been a disappointment to Koani his determination and drive would move his stature to the top in time. As Wahnayah sat playing with his son, Gijook, Ankawoo approached the two. Ankawoo spoke, "He is growing fast and strong. Gijook will make a strong warrior like his father." Then he addressed Wahnayah directly, "I want you to pick a band of warriors to go and raid the Tsimshians. They have stolen several of our slaves and killed one of our warriors while they were out picking berries. We must teach them a lesson."

Wahnayah handed the child to Tikal and nodded. Standing up he faced Ankawoo and told him, "I will leave at first light in the morning." Wahnayah chose eight of the strongest warriors, and then they armed themselves, and would take enough provisions for the journey.

Wahnayah was up before daylight. He picked up Gijook and hugged him and Tikal. She was anxious about his journey—he still walked with a slight limp from the arrow to his hip. No use for her to say anything, it was man's business and not for her to mention. That night she made love to him, it helped to ease her anxiety. He told her it would be early the next morning before they left.

The sun turned the sky a brilliant orange as it peered over the mountain range to the east. Wahnayah motioned for the others to follow him as those outside stood and watched the band disappear as they headed south. The journey would take them at least two days and they would have to be careful not to be spotted. They would hope to surprise the Tsimshians as they slept. They were a small band—this would be a one-chance shot, then they would have to run. All day they traveled slowly moving toward their target, and by late evening Wahnayah found a good place to camp down in a gorge. He would post a guard; he recommended they all get some sleep and be rested for the next day.

The next morning they were up before daylight. Each ate some of the jerky in their bags as they moved on. Wahnayah sent Yaqui ahead to scout as the main group followed moving slow. By late in the evening Yaqui returned; he had spotted the village ahead—they had three guards posted. Wahnayah decided to camp here; they would attack right at daylight.

Two hours before daylight Wahnayah was up early as he woke everyone up. They prepared for battle as each man gave prayer to the Great Spirit to give them victory. Wahnayah covered his face and arms with black from the charcoal in his bag. Slowly they moved ahead, and when they were within a few hundred yards of the camp, Yaqui pointed out where the guards were. Wahnayah instructed Xoot, Yaqui and Naagasei to take out the guards. The rest spread out and waited for signals from the three that the guards were dead. Wahnayah patiently waited, then one by one the signals came—it was time for them to move. Slowly they approached the sleeping village a dog yelped once; he never got a second chance as Wahnayah's arrow silenced the mangy mutt. It was time, with a hair-curling yell Wahnayah signaled that the attack was on.

The Tsimshians were completely taken by surprise—by the time they realized what was going on Wahnayah and his band were on their way back to the Tlingit village. The band had not only taken back the slaves the Tsimshians had captured but three more to add to that group. Wahnayah had not lost a man as they moved quickly away from the village. He knew they would be like a mad swarming bunch of bees. Yaqui lagged back; he would watch to make sure they were not overtaken. By dark they had traveled a long distance from the Tsimshian village Wahnayah signaled for the band to stop. Xoot would guard the slaves while Wahnayah took the first guard and the rest would sleep. They would move on before daylight—he didn't want to be overtaken. Wahnayah instructed Yaqui to feed and water the slaves—he would give them better treatment than he received as a slave.

Before daylight he had them all up and under the twilight of a quarter moon they followed the trail that would lead them to the village. He heard an owl back in the forest calling for a mate as he stopped for a couple of seconds then moved on. They picked up the pace and by noontime they reached their village. Naagasei let out with the sound of an owl and was answered high above in the mountains signifying it was clear for them to enter the village. Koani and the village all turned out to watch as the band entered the village. Ankawoo patted Wahnayah on the back and told him, "Good work," as he walked toward Tikal. She smiled and felt proud and relieved that her man had come home safe to her and Gijook again. It would be a long while before the Tsimshians would want to mess with their village.

Gijook was now going on five years old. Wahnayah watched as Ankawoo worked with him teaching him to shoot his bow and arrows. Every day he was getting stronger and he looked a lot like Wahnayah except he had black hair like his mother. Tikal was pregnant with their second child and told Wahnayah that she would give him another son but down in her heart she wished for a daughter. Tikal was well honored among the women. Munaka, now well along in age, was nearly blind. She depended on Tikal to help her with her magic and potions since she could not see. The old woman knew she needed to pass her secrets on to someone and she trusted Tikal. Wahnayah had mixed feelings when it came to Munaka. She was both an enemy and now a friend who had saved his life. It was sad to see her in this weakened stage of her life. But things change and the day was coming that the women would have a new Munaka. Wahnayah was proud that Tikal had learned Munaka's ways and he knew she would be a good candidate someday to take that position in the tribe.

Koani was ready to take a wife; she would come from the Bear clan. She had been picked for him since he was a youth. Her name was Teinan Geey. His marriage to her would strengthen his status among the Tlingit tribes. Marriage was not always just for love but among the royalty it was used for gaining more power. Koani and Teinan Geey's marriage would be a grand affair. Yakutat had planned this wedding for his son even while Koani was first born. This wise old chief was always thinking ahead and working to keep his power and wealth close to home. Unfortunately he did not live to see this day that his son would marry the woman he had picked for him. The two villages from which the young couple came from had brought these two Tlingit tribes together for this great event. Just as was the case for Wahnayah and Tikal, only on a much greater scale, Koani and Teinan Geey sat in the middle of the large room of the longhouse. Wahnayah and Tikal danced along with many others as they celebrated the marriage of their leader. As the day wore on Tikal was in charge of preparing the marriage hut for the young couple. When the time came it was Ankawoo who led the procession that followed them to the hut. They all cheered as the couple entered the hut, then they returned to the festivities that would last for several days.

As the wedding party was winding down word came by messenger from one of the Tlingit tribes down south. Akado, the messenger, brought word that a skirmish had occurred between his tribe and a great wooden canoe. Something had gone wrong while they were trading with the white men and argument broke out and many of his people had been massacred. The village had been burned to the ground and all valuables had been stolen and carted off by the Spaniards. The Tlingits agreed this could not go unpunished. This would not be the last they would see of these men and their great ships. Wahnayah knew this even better than the rest and the thing he dreaded and had convinced himself would not happen, did happen. Ankawoo consulted with Koani and they decided to call a meeting of all the Tlingits to come and have council on what they should do. A cold chill went down his spine; Wahnayah knew that their weapons were no match for these soldiers with their armor, cannons and rifles. His main concern turned toward his family—Tikal pregnant and Gijook, his son. The village was still astir even as darkness fell and the village settled in to sleep.

A week had passed since the news of the massacre. Other chiefs filtered into the village from up north and south to the council meeting. The sun broke over the mountains when Koani called the council together. Ankawoo and Wahnayah would get to sit in on the meeting. Since Wahnayah was white his words would be important to the group. It had been a long time since he had been in the white man's world; he had no idea how much had changed. To the white man Indians were just ignorant savages. Tikal knew Wahnayah was worried. She did not bother him this morning but fed him his breakfast then left him alone. Soon Xoot came and summoned them to the council hut; it was time for the meeting.

As Ankawoo and Wahnayah entered the smoke-filled room they were instructed to sit at the end of the long line of men in attendance. Koani wore his cedar hat and naxeim, as all the chiefs were well dressed—this was a very important meeting. Much murmuring filled the room then Koani raised his hand to start the meeting. He explained what the meeting was about and then he asked for anyone who might have something to say.

Chumaki stood up and Koani recognized him and told him to talk. Chumaki, an old chief from one of the Tlingit tribes down south, spoke slowly, "We were fishing along the shore of the Great Salt Lake that has no end. We saw something in the distance, it was a large canoe with white wings and we watched as it came closer. We moved into the bank and hid our canoe as we watched it move along the shore. The great canoe came in close to where we hid. We could see men who wore iron clothes, had beards and carried fire sticks. I have never heard the language that these humans spoke. Then the great canoe opened his white wings and moved quickly out into the Great Salt Lake and soon disappeared. When we were convinced it was gone we came out from hiding." Then Chumaki sat down.

Silence filled the room as Chumaki spoke and when he was finished the room was filled with talk. Koani once again raised his hand and the room quieted down. Koani looked at Wahnayah and knew he wanted to know what he had to say. Rising to his feet slowly he stood for a moment searching his mind how to tell them what they had seen. Then Wahnayah began to speak, "Oh my chief Koani! It is of truth I was once a white man as these you have seen. We called this great canoe, a ship. The wings you speak of are called sails that catch the wind and push the great canoe through the waters. This ship has traveled for many moons to reach our shores and they have great fire sticks called cannons. This canoe is very powerful and dangerous to whoever should decide to attack it. These soldiers wear iron clothes that protect them from our arrows. If you are to kill them you must shoot your arrows at their faces. Chumaki and his men did the right thing to hide from these men. I say all Tlingits must avoid any contact with these people. There are many such tribes across the great waters. The Tlingit weapons are no match for their weapons."

A great angry uproar broke out at these words. Akada screamed out, "The Tlingits are no cowards— we must avenge our blood!" Others murmured that Wahnayah was once one of these and that he wished to protect them.

He saw that the truth only angered them so he said, "That is all I have to say on this matter."

He sat back down then Caynuk, a young brave, asked to speak. Koani motioned for him to speak. "I think Wahnayah wants to protect these people from my sharp arrows. Maybe he is still loyal to them. They are only a few, we are many, we could sneak on their large canoe and kill them all." Then he sat down to the agreement of many of the others.

Then Ankawoo motioned and Koani told him to speak. Ankawoo chose his words carefully as he too began to speak slowly, "Wahnayah's honor is not what the discussion is about. He has proven himself many times in battle for our people. His bravery is known by many of us. Perhaps he has a plan in how to rid our land of these humans? This is all I have to say."

No one else attempted to speak, then Koani turned to Daanaa Kaa, who raised his hand to speak. Koani nodded and he began to talk. "I am Daanaa Kaa and I am an old man. Maybe the Great Spirit has chosen to let me live this long for this moment. I have listened to Ankawoo, Caynuk, Wahnayah, Chumaki and others and each has wise council and speaks from his heart. But I know this that this is our land and we must fight or we will lose it. It would be better if we could be friends with these iron men. We only wanted to trade with them and they have made themselves enemies. Let us teach them a lesson that the Tlingit people are strong. We should pick our time to attack. It is better that we perish rather than become slaves. This is what I say."

Then Koani said, "We have heard much to think about." Then he lifted the sacred pipe to the heavens, took a puff and passed the pipe around the room. Wahnayah knew that the old man was right, they would have to fight but the overwhelming numbers were against them.

Wahnayah returned to the longhouse looking for Tikal. He spoke to her about what was discussed in the meeting. He told her the white man's hunger for more land never ceases. She could see the worry in his eyes but she chose not to ask the many questions that burned in her heart. Then he smiled and patted her on the abdomen. She replied, "It is not long now, my husband." He sat down next to her and they ate without another word. In his heart he knew that a very dark storm was hovering over the Tlingits. Life and harmony as they all knew it was about to change forever and there was nothing he or they could do to stop it.

They moved into the winter season, and this was a particularly hard winter for man and beast alike. Wahnayah knew that they had not seen the last of the men and their ships. Chief Koani didn't think they would see these ships and men; after all, they had only been seen by the tribes far south of them. It was not bad enough a fever broke out through the tribe. Munaka had been one of the first to contract the fever, and nothing Tikal could do would save the old woman in her weakened condition. Wahnayah worried that Tikal might catch the fever but she knew many of Munaka's cures and was expected to do what she could. They both worked tirelessly tending to the many who had the fever. There was word that the fever had spread to the other tribes as well. Probably their contact with the white men was where this fever had come from.

Wahnayah knew it was scarlet fever, the same disease that had claimed his mother and father. Several weeks had passed, then Tikal came down with the fever. Wahnayah stayed right by her side; she was burning up and shook from the chills. He was helpless to aid her, then she went into labor and lost their child. Wahnayah wrapped the baby girl in their best blanket and placed it on the fire. He had advised Koani that they should burn the dead. As Tikal slept Ankawoo told Wahnayah that they would be in the prayer hut. Wahnayah joined them. As he entered the hut filled with smoke many were there already praying to the Great Spirit. It was a terrible time for the village, so many had died.

Xoot called Wahnayah from the hut to come fast, running back to the longhouse he found Tikal gasping for air. He sat by her side feeling as helpless as he did with Tahou when he found her in the cabin. Tikal hung to life with an uncanny will to live but finally she gave in. Wahnayah groaned within himself—he had lost two women that he loved. Ankawoo touched his friend on the shoulder; there was nothing he could say or do to help relieve his pain. Wrapping her in his naxeim robe he took her to the burial fire. He was not alone—there was much weeping in the village, as they had lost nearly a third of their population. Some of the tribes had lost even more members than they. Tikal had been a good mother and wife, he would miss her. The emptiness once again filled his heart. The village drums and flutes played the sad music of death. He still had Gijook, his son; they had survived the fever.

Gijook was seven now and as was with the Tlingit tradition he went to live with his uncle Ankawoo for training. Ankawoo and Miwoki took Gijook in and they would train him to be a Tlingit warrior. Gijook would spend most of his time with Ankawoo learning the ways of his people. He would still have contact with his father but Ankawoo would do the teaching. Ankawoo, like Wahnayah, lost a daughter to the terrible fever. They had no other children. Wahnayah knew that his friend could teach his son as well as he to be a man and a Tlingit. Even though it was hard he would honor their ways—he had vowed to be a Tlingit.

Many years passed and Wahnayah watched as his son grew stronger. The fever had greatly diminished their numbers, and it was difficult to have the type of potlatches that they'd had in the past. The Tlingits had bigger problems, more severe than preparing for the potlatches or dealing with the fever. The iron men had returned to the coast down south and the word came up that they had completely wiped out one of the Tlingit villages. The Tlingits enjoyed taking things from others and did not consider it stealing since everything belonged to everyone. When confronted they would quickly return the item to its owner. This had caused the friction between the iron men and Tlingits. Gathering together, the Tlingits decided to teach the iron men a lesson. A large group of them swam out to the ship at night. A small crew was onboard as the majority of the men were trading on the shore. They boarded the ship, surprising the crew and killing them, and then they set fire to the ship. Those on shore that were trading were completely overtaken by the numbers and all were killed in a surprise attack. The Tlingits thought this would cure their problem with the iron men but Wahnayah knew they had no idea what they had done. That would only exacerbate the problem—many men would come with guns and ships and avenge their shipmates.

Then one day while Wahnayah and a group of warriors were hunting near the coast for seals they spotted a whaleboat. Alarmed he ordered all of them to flee back into the forest for cover. It was too late, they had been spotted, and as they ran for cover the iron men opened fire on the hunting party. Three of his hunting party fell dead as the bullets found their target. Wahnayah was the only one who had a rifle. Taking aim with his Hawkens he dropped one with a bullet to the head. The young warriors wanted to make a stand, but he knew they were outgunned and he ordered them to go to the village. Reloading, he moved through the forest then took aim and dropped another. The iron men grabbing their dead retreated to the canoe and left. Once Wahnayah was sure they were gone he followed the others back to the village.

When he reached the village a great multitude protesting his decision met him. The young warriors were angry and accused him of being a coward. Then Koani took control of the situation and called a council meeting to discuss what had really happened. Pocoma stood up angrily and began to speak. He told the others of how they were hunting when they came upon a boat on the bank. Wahnayah yelled for all of them to run for the forest and while they were doing that the iron men started firing on them. Pocoma said that they should have taken them on but Wahnayah wanted them to retreat. As they ran for cover three of them were killed. Angrily he sat down pointing his finger at Wahnayah.

Then Koani motioned for Wahnayah to stand up and speak. Wahnayah told them what Pocoma said was true. He said, "Pocoma is a courageous warrior but our weapons were no match for theirs. I was trying to save as many of the lives in our party as I could and am sorry we lost three of our best warriors. My Hawkens was the only weapon that had a chance against the iron men. If I hadn't had my rifle we would have all been killed but I managed to kill two of the iron men while the others escaped. I saw them jump into their boat and leave carrying the two I killed with them." Pocoma then shouted out that he did not see any dead iron men, that, that was a lie. Wahnayah then continued, "I know that Pocoma wanted to avenge his dead brothers but Pocoma would be dead now if we had done any different." Then he said, "They will come again. We must be ready to fight them. That is all I have to say."

Koani then spoke, "Does anyone else have something to say?" No one spoke then Koani replied, "It is late. We will talk about this matter more." Then the meeting broke up and all returned to the longhouse. The young brave Pocoma, still fuming, stared hard at Wahnayah but said nothing else.

Several years had passed and everyone forgot about the iron men. The iron men were actually Russians and this time they came with three ships, several small cannons and a hundred and fifty soldiers. The Russians made friends with the Kutchins, who warred with the Tlingits from time to time. Under the cover of darkness they moved down the river and found the village nestled in the mountains. Their intentions were to build a fort in the area to protect their interests. They canoed up the river into the creek, then the Kutchins took out the Tlingit guards under darkness. They quietly positioned their cannons on the mountaintops; they would hit the village at daybreak.

Wahnayah couldn't sleep. He got up and wandered outside and sat down next to the totem pole. Then he heard an owl in the distance. This alarmed him. He looked and couldn't see any of the guards in the twilight of the moon. Something was going on. He quietly went back into the longhouse and picked up his Hawkens. Outside he went into the forest and quietly moved up the hill toward where Pocoma was standing guard. As he neared the position he spotted one of the iron men manning a cannon. A cold chill of fear ran up and down his spine. They were preparing to attack the village—he must warn the others. Sneaking back down the mountain he entered the longhouse and went straight to Koani's room, rapping on the door.

The word was quickly spread through the village, but before the village was prepared the cannons went off, sending hot steel crashing into the longhouse. The longhouse only had the single door in front—they were trapped. A cannon ball blew a hole in the chief's room, killing his wife instantly. The chief, badly wounded, crawled out through the hole in the wall and was cut down by gunfire.

Wahnayah grabbed his Hawkens and pistol and squatted down peering through the door. A large pile of those who ran through the door lay dead. Frantically looking for Gijook he spotted him near the fire and waved for him to come. There was no chance of going out the door without getting a bullet. Grabbing Gijook by the arm they made their way to the hole in the wall where Koani lay dead. Looking through the hole in the wall he spotted two snipers gunning down anyone who attempted to come through the hole. Taking aim he squeezed the trigger on the Hawkens and a soldier fell back as his bullet blew the top of his head off. Pulling Gijook down under him as a cannon ball hit the front door blowing splinters all through the room.

There was death everywhere—some were young children, some were groaning from wounds. The only thing he could think of was trying to save Gijook's life. Loading his Hawkens he peered through the hole. The only soldier left was bent over his friend. Taking aim he dropped that one also. Grabbing Gijook he jumped through the hole with pistol drawn. Handing Gijook his knife he told him to run for the forest. Then Wahnayah watched as the boy disappeared into the woods. Another soldier hidden started to follow Gijook and Wahnayah dropped him with a shot to the back of his head. With Gijook out of sight Wahnayah worked his way along the wall toward the front of the longhouse. Bodies and blood covered the entire courtyard. Then he spotted Ankawoo sitting against the totem pole; he was mortally wounded. He had to help his friend. Firing his Hawkens he dropped another soldier who was readying his bayonet to finish off Ankawoo. Then he felt a burn to his left shoulder as a bullet knocked him backwards and then fell to his knees. Looking up, a group of soldiers was running toward him with bayonets flashing. Firing his pistol rapidly four of the soldiers collapsed, then he used his rifle as a club as he struggled to his feet. A cannon ball hit close, knocking him off of his feet and momentarily stunning him. Glancing toward his friend Ankawoo he could see the cannon ball nearly cut him in half. The soldiers were now running through the village shooting and stabbing everyone they could. As they closed in on him he fired his remaining two shots from his pistol, dropping two more. Then he was overwhelmed with his wounds and loss of blood and fell to the ground face down. Slowly darkness closed in on him as he prayed that Gijook had escaped.

Gijook ran into the forest, he dove over a dead tree stump as a bullet whizzed past his head. He heard another shot and peering over the tree he spotted the soldier collapse; he knew his father had dropped this one. The young boy remembered what Ankawoo had taught him as he dug out a hole under the fallen tree. Crawling under he covered himself up with dirt and leaves. His arm was burning he felt and realized a bullet had nicked him. Too scared to move he could hear rifles firing and the occasional terrible thunder of the cannons that made him jump each time. Tears came to his eyes at the remembrance of the terrible things his young eyes had seen at the village. After several hours the noise of the battle began to subside. Once he heard soldiers hunting for survivors in the forest but he lay very still and they overlooked him. As darkness began to fall across the valley Gijook shivered from the cool night air. An owl hooted deep in the forest. He wanted to come out and look for his father but he knew better than to do that.

Very late into the night when he felt it was safe he brushed away the leaves and crawled out from his hiding place. Feeling the wound on his shoulder he could tell it had scabbed over and stopped bleeding. Sitting back against the log he looked up into a starry sky. He must move further away from the village in the dark, it was not safe here. Following an animal trail through the forest he slowly climbed a mountain that led out of the valley. He came upon a small stream that flowed from the mountain. Bending down in the dark he cupped some of the water and drank it, quenching his dry thirsty lips. He washed his wound then took his bandana and wrapped it around the wound. For a moment he sat listening hoping he would hear someone else who might have escaped. In his thoughts he knew he must be a man now, he had to be brave.

Just before daylight he reached the summit of the mountain. A large boulder stuck out which he hid behind. Looking below he could see the village in the distance. Smoke rose up over what was once the longhouse that was his home. A large fire was burning in the center of the village. What he saw made him vomit. The soldiers had piled a large number of bodies near the fire. A hatred for these people filled his heart for what they had done to his people. All he had of his father was his knife tucked in his buckskin pants. He knew his father and all his people were dead. Then his father's last words came to his mind, "Go north, son. Save yourself to fight another day." Those were the last words his father said as he pushed him toward the forest. He remembered his father had warned him and his mother that one day the white man might come. Who would push the Tlingits from their land? They had always lived there, and hadn't many others tried to take it? They were too strong for that to ever happen, he thought.

The young boy's eye caught sight of a lone eagle as it flew north across the mountain. Checking the sun he took a deep breath and turned his face north. Follow the eagle, be brave—that was what he would do. One last glance toward the village, under his breath he said farewell to the people and village he loved. He would move north and look for another Tlingit village; he would warn them so they could help him run these Windigos from his village. A tear fell from his cheek. He was a Tlingit warrior, he would return. He would avenge his father and his people, he would bring honor to his people. Gijook dropped off the mountain as he moved on north. A cool wind blew in his face; he knew that winter would be coming soon. The eagle's wings caught in the wind as he circled, then dropped out of the sky into the valley. Gijook wished he could fly like the great eagle; there must be a large body of water over there, he thought.

Bibliography

Barnard, Edward S. *Story of the Great American West.* Pleasantville, NY: Reader's Digest Association Inc,1977.

Maxwell, James A., ed. *America's Fascinating Indian Heritage.* Pleasantville, NY: Reader's Digest Association Inc,1978.

Web pages:

Tlingit

Encyclopedia of North American Indians
http://college.hmco.com/history/readerscomp/naind/html/na_039100_tlingit.htm

Haida

Encyclopedia of North American Indians
http://college.hmco.com/history/readerscomp/naind/html/na_013900_haida.htm

Tsimshian

Wikipedia The Free Encyclopedia
http://en.wikipedia.org/wiki/tsimshian

Kwakiutl

Encyclopedia of North American Indians
http://college.hmco.com/history/readerscomp/naind/html/na_019100_kwakiutl.htm

Nootka
Wikipedia The Free Encyclopedia
http://en.wikipedia.org/wiki/Nootka

Ojibwa
Encyclopedia of North American Indians
http://college.hmco.com/history/readerscomp/naind/html/na_026100_ojibwa.htm

Breinigsville, PA USA
02 September 2009
223481BV00001B/32/A

9 781413 795523